Mary Elizabeth Braddon

A Strange World

A novel. Part 3

Mary Elizabeth Braddon

A Strange World
A novel. Part 3

ISBN/EAN: 9783337050603

Printed in Europe, USA, Canada, Australia, Japan

Cover: Foto ©Andreas Hilbeck / pixelio.de

More available books at **www.hansebooks.com**

A STRANGE WORLD

A Novel

BY THE AUTHOR OF

'LADY AUDLEY'S SECRET'

ETC. ETC. ETC.

IN THREE VOLUMES

VOL. III.

LONDON

JOHN MAXWELL AND CO.

4, SHOE LANE, FLEET STREET

1875

CONTENTS TO VOL. III.

CHAP.		PAGE
I.	'LOST TO HER PLACE AND NAME'	I
II.	'THOU HAST ALL SEASONS FOR THINE OWN, O DEATH!'	53
III.	FIRE THAT IS CLOSEST KEPT BURNS MOST OF ALL	66
IV.	FOR THERE'S NO SAFETY IN THE REALM FOR ME	78
V.	'FOR THOU WERT STILL THE POOR MAN'S STAY'	94
VI.	I FOUND HIM GARRULOUSLY GIVEN	104
VII.	'FULL COLD MY GREETING WAS AND DRY'	122
VIII.	'WHEN TIME SHALL SERVE, BE THOU NOT SLACK'	129
IX.	'THE DAYS HAVE VANISHED, TONE AND TINT'	152
X.	'THE SADDEST LOVE HAS SOME SWEET MEMORY	183
XI.	'STABB'D THROUGH THE HEART'S AFFECTIONS TO THE HEART'	193
XII.	'IT IS TIME, O PASSIONATE HEART,' SAID I	215
XIII.	'NOT AS A CHILD SHALL WE AGAIN BEHOLD HER'	227
XIV.	'A SOUL AS WHITE AS HEAVEN'	236
XV.	ENID, THE PILOT, STAR OF MY LONE LIFE	259
XVI.	'FOR ALL IS DARK WHERE THOU ART NOT'	282
XVII.	'BUT IN SOME WISE ALL THINGS WEAR ROUND BETIMES'	289

A STRANGE WORLD

CHAPTER I.

HAVING come to Borcel End to perform a certain duty, Maurice Clissold gave himself up heart and soul to the task in hand. Pleasant as it might have been to him to spend the greater part of his time in the agreeable society of Mrs. Penwyn and her guests —playing croquet on sunny afternoons, or joining in a match of billiards in the old hall, meeting the best people to be met in that part of the world, and living that smooth, smiling life, in which care seems to have no part—pleasant as this might have been, he gave it up without a sigh, and spent his days and nights strolling about the farm, or sitting by the hearth where the sick woman's presence maintained an unchanging gloom.

VOL. III.   B

Every day showed the swift progress of disease. The malady, which had made its first approaches with insidious slowness, was now advancing upon the sufferer with appalling rapidity. Every day the hectic of the dying woman's cheek took a more feverish brightness, the glassy eye a more awful light. Maurice felt that there was no time to be lost. His eyes, less accustomed to the aspect of the invalid than the eyes of kindred who had seen her daily throughout the progress of decline, clearly perceived that the end was not far off. Whatever secrets were hidden in that proud heart must be speedily revealed, or would remain buried there till the end of time. Yet how was he, almost a stranger, to win confidence which had been refused to a son?

He tried his uttermost to conciliate Mrs. Trevanard by small attentions. He adjusted the window-curtains, so as to temper the light for those weary eyes. He arranged the invalid's pillow as tenderly as Martin could have done. He read to her—sometimes reading passages of Scripture which she herself selected, and which were frequently of an awful and denunciatory character, the cry of prophets and holy men against the iniquities of their age.

Those portions of Holy Writ which he himself chose were of a widely different tone. He read all that is most consoling, most tender in the Gospel. The words he chose were verily messengers of peace. And even that stubborn heart was touched—the woman who had prided herself on her own righteousness felt that she was a sinner.

One afternoon when Maurice and Mrs. Trevanard were alone by the fireside—Martin and his father being both at Seacomb market, and old Mrs. Trevanard being confined to her own room with a sharp attack of rheumatism—the invalid appeared struck by the young man's kindness in remaining with her.

' I should be dull company for you at the best of times,' she said, ' and it's worse for you now that I'm so ill. Why don't you go for a ride or a drive, and enjoy the country, instead of sitting in this dismal room with me ? '

' I am very glad to keep you company, Mrs. Trevanard,' he answered, kindly. ' You must find time heavy on market days, when there's no one here.'

'Yes, the hours seem very long. I make one of the girls sit here at her needlework. But that's almost worse than loneliness, to hear the click, click, click of the needle, and see the girl sitting there, with no more sense in her than a statue, or not so much, for a statue does no harm. And then one gets thinking of the past, and the things we have done which we ought not to have done, and the things left undone which we ought to have done. It's a dreary thought. When I was well and strong, and able to bustle about the house, I used to think I had done my duty in that state of life to which it had pleased God to call me. I knew that I had never spared myself, or given myself up to the lusts of the flesh, such as eating, and drinking, and slothfulness. The hardest crust or the poorest bit off the joint was always good enough for me. I was always the first up of a morning, summer and winter, and my hands were never idle. But since I've been ill, and sitting here all day, I've come to think myself a sinner. That's a hard thought, Mr. Clissold, after a life of care and labour.'

Perhaps it is the best thought any of us can

have,' he answered, 'the natural conclusion of every Christian who considers how far his highest endeavours fall short of his Master's divine example Remember the story of the publican.'

And then he read that sublimely simple record of the two men who went up into the temple to pray.

He had hardly finished when Mrs. Trevanard burst into tears, the first he had ever seen her shed. The sight shocked him, and yet inspired hope.

'I have been like the Pharisee, I have trusted in my own righteousness,' she said at last, drying her tears.

'Dear Mrs. Trevanard,' Maurice began, earnestly, 'there are few of us altogether blameless—there are few lives in which some wrong has not been done to others—some mistake made which, perhaps, has gone far to wreck the happiness of others. The uttermost we can do, the uttermost God will demand from us, is repentance and atonement—such poor atonement, at least, as we may be able to offer for the wrong we have done. But it is a

bitter thing to outstand God's hour, and hold by
our wrong-doing, to appear before Him as obstinate
sinners who know their sin, yet cleave to it.'

The words moved her, for she turned her
face away from him, and buried it on her pillow·
He could see the feeble frame shaken by stifled
sobs.

'If you have wronged any one, and seek to atone
for that wrong now in this eleventh hour——' said
Maurice.

Mrs. Trevanard turned quickly round, inter-
rupting him. 'Eleventh hour,' she repeated.
'Then they have all made up their minds that
I am to die?'

'Indeed, no! Your husband and son, and all
about you, most earnestly desire your recovery.
But you have been so long suffering from this
trying disease, without improvement, that a natural
fear has arisen——"

'They are right,' she said, with a gloomy look.
'I feel that my doom is upon me.'

'It will not shorten your days, or lessen your
chances of recovery, if you prepare for the worst,

Mrs. Trevanard,' said Maurice, determined to push the question to its ultimate issue. 'Many a man defers making his will, from a dim notion that to make it is to bring death nearer to him; and then some day death approaches him unawares, and his wishes remain unfulfilled. We must all die; so why should we not live prepared for death?'

'I thought I was prepared,' replied Mrs. Trevanard, 'because I have clung to the Scriptures.'

'The Gospel imposes certain duties upon us, and if those duties are unfulfilled our holding by the Bible will avail us very little. It isn't reading the Bible, but living according to its teaching, that will make us Christians.'

'You talk to me boldly,' said the sick woman, 'as if you knew I was a sinner.'

'I know nothing about you, Mrs. Trevanard—except that you seem to have been a good wife and a good mother.'

At that word mother, Bridget Trevanard winced, as if an old wound had been touched.

'But I believe that you have some heavy burden on your mind,' continued Maurice, 'and that you will know neither rest nor peace until that load has been lightened.'

'You are a shrewd judge,' said Mrs. Trevanard, bitterly. 'And pray how came you to think this of me?'

'The conviction has grown out of various circum, stances, which I need not trouble you with. I am a student of mankind, Mrs. Trevanard, a close observer by habit. Pray do not suppose that I have watched you, or played the spy at your fireside. Be assured that I have no feeling but friendship towards you, that my sympathy is ready for your sorrows. And if you can be induced to trust me——'

'If I could trust you!' repeated Mrs. Trevanard. 'If there was any one on earth I dared trust, in whose honest friendship I could believe, in whose word I dare confide the honour of a most unhappy household, heaven knows I would turn to him gladly enough. My husband is weak and helpless, a man who would blab a bitter secret to every acquaintance he has, who would look to [others to drag him out of every difficulty, and make his trouble town-talk. My son is hot-headed and impulsive, would take trouble too deeply to heart, and would be betrayed into some act of folly before I was cold in my grave. No, there are none of my own household I dare trust.'

'Trust me, Mrs. Trevanard.'

She looked at him earnestly with her melancholy eyes—looked as if she would fain have pierced the secrets of his heart.

'You are a man of the world,' she said, 'and therefore might be able to give help and counsel in a difficult matter. You are a gentleman, and therefore would not betray a family secret. But what reason can you have for interesting yourself in my affairs? Why should you take any trouble about me or mine?'

'First, because I am honestly attached to your son; and secondly, because I have felt a profound interest in your afflicted daughter.'

At that word the mother started up from her reclining position, and looked at the speaker fixedly.

'Muriel!' she exclaimed, 'I did not know you had ever seen her.'

'I have seen her and spoken to her. I met her one evening in the copse at the bottom of the garden, and talked to her.'

'What did she talk about?'

'You—and—her child.'

This was a random shot, but it hit the mark.

'Great heaven! she spoke to you of that? A secret of years gone by, which it has been the business of my life to hide; which I have thought of through many a wakeful night upon my weary pillow. And she told you—a stranger?'

'I spoke to her about you, but at the word mother she shrank from me with a look of horror. "Do not speak to me of my mother," she cried, "what has she done with my child?" That speech made a profound impression upon me, as you may imagine. The remembrance of that speech emboldens me to ask for your confidence to-day.'

'I saved that unhappy girl's good name,' said Mrs. Trevanard.

'There you doubtless did a mother's duty. But

was it the maintenance of her character which occasioned the loss of her reason?'

'I don't know. It is a miserable story from first to last. But since you know so much I may as well trust you with the rest; and if, when you have heard all, you think there has been a wrong done that needs redress, you will perhaps help me to bring about that redress.'

'Be assured of my uttermost help, if you will but trust me fully.'

'You shall hear all,' said Mrs. Trevanard, decisively. She took a little of some cooling drink which always stood ready for her on the table by her easy chair, and then began the story of a family sorrow.

'You have seen Muriel,' she said, 'and you have perceived in her wasted countenance some faint traces of former beauty. At eighteen years of age she was a noble creature. She had a face which pleased and attracted every one who saw her. Her schoolmistress wrote me letters about the admiration she had excited on the breaking-up day, when the gentry, whose daughters attended the school, met to witness the distribution of prizes. I was weak enough to shed tears of joy over those letters—weak enough to be proud of gifts which were destined to become a snare of the evil one. Muriel was clever as well as beautiful. She was always at the top of her class, always the winner of prizes. Her father and I used to read her letters again and again, and I think we both worked all the harder, looking forward to the day when Muriel would marry some gentleman farmer, and would require a handsome portion. We were quite content with our own position as simple working people, but we had given Muriel the education of a lady, and we counted upon her marrying above her station.

'"After all, she's a Trevanard," her father used to say, "and the Trevanards come of as good a stock as any in Cornwall—not even barring the Penwyns."

'Well, the time came for Muriel to come home for good. She had not spent much of her holidays at home, for there 'd almost always been some of her favourite fellow-pupils that wanted her company, and when she was invited to stay at gentlefolks' houses I didn't like to say no, and her father said it

was a good thing for her to make friends among the
gentry.   So most of her holiday time had been
spent out visiting, in spite of old Mrs. Trevanard,
who was always grumbling about it, and saying
that no good ever came of people forgetting their
position.   But now the time had come for Muriel to
take her place beside the family hearth, and share
our plain quiet life.'

The mother paused, with a bitter sigh, vividly
recalling that bygone day, and her daughter's
vanished beauty—the fair young face which had
smiled at her from the other side of the hearth,
the happy girlish laugh, the glad young voice,
the atmosphere of youth and brightness which
Muriel's return had brought to the grave old homestead.

'Her grandmother had declared that Muriel
would be dull and discontented at home, that we
had made a great mistake in having her educated
and brought up among her superiors in station,
spoiling her by putting false notions in her head,
and a good deal more of the same kind.   But there
was no discontent about Muriel when she came

among us. She took her place as naturally as possible, wanted to help me with the dairy, or about the house, or to do anything she could to make herself useful. But I was too proud of her beauty and her cleverness to allow that. "No, Muriel," I said, "you've been educated as a lady, and you shall not be the less a lady because you've come home. Your life here may be very dull, there's no help for that, but it shall be the life of a lady. You may play the piano, and read your books, and do fancy work, and no one shall ever call upon you to soil your fingers in dairy work or house work." So when she found I was determined, she gave way and lived like a lady. Her father bought her a piano, which still stands in the best parlour. Her gave her money to buy all the books she wanted. Indeed, there's nothing she could have asked of him that he would have denied her, he was so proud and fond of his only daughter.'

'She brought you happiness, then, in the beginning?' said Maurice.

'Yes, there couldn't have been a better girl than Muriel was for the first year after she left school.

She was always the same sweet smiling creature, full of life, never finding the old house dull, amusing herself day after day with her books and piano, roaming about the fields, and along the beach for hours together, sometimes alone, sometimes with her little brother to keep her company.'

'She was very fond of her brother, I understand?'

'Yes, she doted upon Martin. She taught him to read, and write, and cipher, and used to tell him fairy tales of an evening, between the lights, sitting in a low chair by the hearth. She sang him to sleep many a night. In fact, she took all the trouble of him off my hands. She and her grandmother got on very well together, too, and the old lady having nothing to do, Muriel and she were often companions. Mrs. Trevanard was not blind at that time, but her sight was weak, and she was glad to get Muriel to read to her. Altogether our home seemed brighter and happier after Muriel came back to us. Perhaps we were not humble enough, or thankful enough for our happiness. Anyhow, trouble soon came.'

' How did the evil begin ? '

' As it almost always does. It stole upon us
unawares, iike a thief in the night. The Squire's
eldest son, Captain Penwyn, came home on leave, before going on foreign service with his regiment, and
spent a good deal of his leisure time fly-fishing in
the streams about here. It was splendid summer
weather, and we weren't surprised at his being about
the place so much, especially as folks said that he
and his father didn't get on well together. Now and
again he would come in on a warm afternoon and
take a draught of milk, and sit and talk for half an
hour or so. He was a perfect gentleman, or had the
seeming of one. He was grave and thoughtful in his
ways, yet full of kindness and pleasantness. He
was just the last kind of man that any father and
mother would have thought of shutting their door
against. His manner to Muriel was as respectful
as if she had been the greatest lady in the land, but
he and she naturally found a good deal to say to each
other, she having been educated as a lady, and being
able to understand and appreciate all he said.'

Mrs. Trevanard paused. She was approaching

the painful part of her story, and had need to nerve herself for the effort.

'Heaven knows, I had neither fear nor thought of fear at the **time** our sorrow came upon us. I had complete confidence in Muriel. If I had seen her surrounded by a score of admirers I should have felt no anxiety. She was a **Trevanard**, and the Trevanards had always been noted for beauty and pride. No female of **the** Trevanard family had **ever been** known to lower herself, or to forfeit **her** good name. **And she came of as good** a race **on her mother's side. The last thing I** should have thought of was that **my** daughter would degrade herself by listening to a dishonourable proposal. Well, time went on, and one day Muriel brought **me** a letter she had received **from** her late schoolmistress, asking her to go and stay at the school for a **week or** two at Michaelmas. **The** school was just outside Seacomb, **a** handsome **house,** standing in its own gardens, and there **were** very few of the pupils that were not gentlemen's daughters, **or** at any rate daughters of the richest farmers **in the** neighbourhood. Altogether, Miss Barlow's school stood very high in people's estimation, and I felt flattered by Miss Barlow's asking my daughter to visit her, now that Muriel's schooling days were over, and there was no more money to be expected from us.'

Again a pause and a sigh, and a few minutes of thoughtful silence, before Mrs. Trevanard resumed.

'Muriel was very much excited about the invitation. I remember the bright flush upon her cheeks as she showed me the letter, and her curious, half-breathless way when she asked if I would let her go, and if I thought her father would consent to her going. "Why, you're very anxious to run away from us, Muriel," I said, "but that's only to be expected : Borcel End must be dull for you." "No, indeed, mother," she answered quickly, "Borcel End is a dear old place, and I've been very happy here; but I should like to accept Miss Barlow's invitation."'

'You consented, I suppose?' said Maurice.

'Yes, it wouldn't have been easy for us to refuse anything she asked, at that time. And I think both her father and I were proud of her being made a friend of by such a superior person as Miss

Barlow. So one sunny morning, at the beginning of the Michaelmas holidays, my husband drove Muriel over to Seacomb in the trap, and left her with Miss Barlow. She was to stay a fortnight, and her father was to fetch her at the end of the visit; but before the fortnight was over we had a letter from Muriel, asking to be allowed to extend her visit to three weeks, and saying that her father needn't trouble about fetching her, as Miss Barlow would arrange for sending her home. This wounded Michael a little, being so proud of his daughter. "1 thought my girl would have been glad to see her father after a fortnight's separation," he said. "She always used to be glad when I went over to see her on market days; and if I missed a week she used to call me unkind, and tell me how she had fretted at not seeing me; but I suppose things are changed now she's a young woman."'

'Did she come back at the time promised?'

'No, it was two or three days over the three weeks when she returned. She came in a hired fly from Seacomb, and I had never seen her look more beautiful or more a lady than she looked when she stepped out of the carriage in front of the porch. "Ah," I thought to myself, " she looks as if she was born to hold a high position in the county;" and I thought of Captain Penwyn, and what a match he would be for her. I did not think he was a bit too good for her. "There's no knowing what may happen," I said to myself. Well, from this time forward she had a strange fitful way with her, sometimes all brightness and happiness, sometimes low-spirited. Her grandmother noticed the change, and said it was the consequence of over-education. " You've reared up your child to have all kinds of wishes and fancies that you can't understand or satisfy," she said, "and have made her unfit for her home." I wouldn't believe this ; yet, as time went on, I could see clearly enough that Muriel was not happy.'

Again a heavy sigh, and a brief pause.

' Captain Penwyn left Cornwall about this time, to join his regiment in Canada, and after he had gone, I observed that Muriel's low spirits, which had been fitful before, became continual. She evidently struggled with her grief, tried to amuse herself with her books and piano, tried to interest herself in little Martin, but it was no use. I have often gone into the best parlour where she sat, and found her in tears. I have asked her the cause of her despondency, but she always put me off with some answer: she had been reading a book that affected her, or she had been playing a piece of music which always made her cry; and I noticed that at this time she rarely played any music that was not melancholy. If she began anything bright and gay, she always broke down in it, and her father sometimes asked her what had become of all her lively tunes. All at once it struck me that perhaps she had grown attached to Captain Penwyn, little as they had seen of each other, and that she was fretting at his absence. Yet I thought this would be too foolish for our Muriel. Or perhaps she had been wounded by his indifference to her. A girl accustomed to so much admiration as she had received might expect to make conquests. I used to puzzle myself about the cause of her sadness for hours together as I went about the house, but in all my thoughts of Muriel, I never imagined anything near the horrible truth.'

She stopped, clasped her hands before her face, and then went on hurriedly. 'One night, when Muriel was sitting by this hearth, with her brother in her arms, singing to him, she broke down suddenly, and began to sob hysterically. Her father was frightened out of his wits, and came fussing about her in a way to make her worse, but I put my arm round her and led her to her own room. When we were together there she flung herself upon my breast, and then the awful truth came out. A child was to be born in this house—a child whose birth must be hidden, whose father's name was never to be spoken.'

'Did she tell you all the truth?'

'She told me nothing. There was a secret, she said—a secret she had solemnly sworn to keep, come what might. She asked me to trust her, to believe in her honour, in spite of all that seemed to condemn her. She asked me to send her away somewhere, to some quiet corner of the earth where no one need know her name or anything about her.

But I told her there was no corner of the earth so secret that slander and shame would not follow her, and no hiding-place so safe as her father's house. "If you were to go away it would set people talking," I said.'

'There may have been a secret marriage,' suggested Maurice.

'I asked her that question, but she refused to answer. I cannot believe that she would have kept back the truth from me, her mother, in that hour of agony. I asked her if George Penwyn was the villain who had brought this misery upon us, but this question also she refused to answer. She had made a promise that sealed her lips, she said. I must think the worst of her, if I could not trust her.'

'Would it not have been better and wiser to believe in your daughter's honour, even in the face of circumstances that seemed to condemn?' asked Maurice, with a touch of reproach.

'Who can be wise when they see all they have most loved and honoured suddenly snatched away from them? The discovery of my daughter's dishonour was more bitter to me than her sudden death would have been. When I left her that night my prayer was that she might die, and her sorrow and her blighted name go down unknown to the grave. A wicked prayer, you think, no doubt; but you have never passed through such an agony as I felt that night. I lay awake thinking what was to be done. I had no doubt in my own mind that George Penwyn was the man who had slain my daughter's soul. There was no one else I could suspect. When I rose at daybreak next morning I had my plan, in some measure, settled.'

Maurice listened breathlessly; he felt that he was on the threshold of the household mystery—the sacrifice that had been made to the family's good name.

'Whenever any of us were ill, old Mrs. Trevanard used to doctor us. She has all kinds of recipes for medicines to cure small ailments. It was only when a case was very bad that we sent for a doctor. Now my first precaution was to remove Muriel to the room above her grandmother's, a room cut off from the rest of the house, as you know, and to place her under old Mrs. Trevanard's care, in such a manner that the house-servant—we had only one then—had no chance of approaching her. To do this, of course I had to tell Mrs. Trevanard the secret. You may suppose that went hard with me, but the old lady behaved well throughout my trouble, and never spoke a reproachful word of Muriel. "Let her come to me, poor lamb," she said, "I'll stand by her, come what may." So we moved Muriel to that out-of-the-way room, and I told her father that she was ill with a slight attack of low fever, and that I thought it wisest to place her in her grandmother's care. He was very anxious and fidgety about her, and a dreadful gloom seemed to fall upon the house. I know that I went about my daily work with a heart that was ready to break.'

'It must have been a hard time, indeed,' said Maurice, compassionately.

'It was so hard as to try my faith in God's goodness. My heart rebelled against His decrees; but just when my despair was deepest, Providence seemed to come to my help in a most unlooked-for manner. It was winter at this time, near the end of winter, and very severe weather The moors were covered with snow, and no one came near Borcel from one week's end to another. One evening about dusk I was leaving the dairy, which is detached from the house, and crossing the yard to go back to the kitchen, when I saw a man and woman looking over the yard gate, the snow beating down upon them—two as miserable objects as you could see. My heart was hardened against others by my own grief, so I called to them to go away, I had nothing to give them.

'"If we go away from here it will be to certain death," answered the man. "As you are a Christian, give us a night's shelter. We left Seacomb early this morning to walk to Penwyn Manor, having a letter recommending us to the Squire's charity ; but the walk was longer and more difficult than we knew, and here we are at dark, just halfway on our journey. I don't ask much from you,—only enough to save us from perishing—a night's lodging in one of your empty barns."

'This was an appeal I could not resist. There was room enough to have sheltered twenty such

wanderers. So I took these two up to a hayloft
that was seldom used, and gave them a truss of old
hay for a bed; and I carried them a loaf and a jug
of milk with my own hands. I don't know what
put it into my head to wait upon them myself,
instead of sending the servant to them, but I think
it pleased me to do this humble office, knowing how
low my daughter had fallen, and feeling as if there
were some kind of atonement in my humility.

'These people were not common wanderers. I
soon discovered that they were very different from
the tramps who came prowling about the place in
summer, begging or stealing whenever they had a
chance. The woman was a pretty-looking, gentle
creature, who seemed deeply grateful for small kindnesses. She had not long recovered from a serious
illness, the husband told me, and her delicate looks
confirmed his statement. The man spoke well, if
not exactly like a gentleman, and his clothes, though
worn almost to rags, were not the clothes of a
working man. I fancied that he was a lawyer's
clerk, or perhaps, from his fluency of speech, a
broken-down Methodist parson.'

' He spoke like a man accustomed to speaking in public, then, I conclude,' said Maurice.

'Yes, that was the impression he gave me,' replied Mrs. Trevanard. 'I went back to the house after having made them tolerably comfortable in the loft,' she continued, 'and all that night I lay awake thinking about these two people. They seemed to have dropped from the skies, somehow, so suddenly and unexpectedly had they come upon me in the winter dusk; and it came into my head, in that weary night, that they were instruments of Providence sent to help me in my trouble. I had no clear thought of what they would do for me, but I felt that since I should be compelled to trust some one, by and by, with some part of our fatal secret, it would be easier and better to trust waifs and strays like these, who might wander away and carry their knowledge with them, than anybody else. Neighbour or friend I dared not trust. My sole hope lay among strangers.'

'Did none of the farm people know of these wanderers' arrival?' asked Maurice.

'No. The men were at their supper when I took these people to the loft. It was a loft over an empty stable, and was only used at odd times for a surplus supply of fodder. I knew it was safe enough as a hiding-place, so long as the people kept tolerably quiet. I had warned them against making their presence known, as my husband was a hard man—heaven forgive me for so great a falsehood— and might object to their being about the place. Well, the snow came down thicker than ever next morning, and to try and find a path across the moor would have been madness. Those most accustomed to the country round would have been helpless in such weather. So I took the people in the loft a warm comfortable breakfast of coffee and bread and bacon, and I told them that they might stay till the weather changed.'

'They were grateful, I suppose.'

'They thanked and blessed me, with tears. I was ashamed to receive their thanks, knowing my selfish thought had been only of my own trouble, and how little I had cared for their distress. The man told me that his name was Eden, and that he was a broken-down gentleman. I think he said he had been in the army, and had wealthy relations, but they had discarded him, and after trying to earn his living by the use of his talents, he had fallen into extreme poverty. He and his wife had come to Cornwall, having heard that living was cheap in the west of England. I gathered from him that he had tried to pick up a living by teaching, but had failed, and was at last compelled to leave his lodgings, and in his extremity had determined to appeal to Squire Penwyn, whom he had heard of as a wealthy man. For that purpose he had rashly attempted to walk across the moor, the snow having held off for a little, with his weakly wife. "Heaven help you if you had found your way to the old Squire!" I told him. "He's not the man to do much for you." I told them both that they might stay until the weather was better, or stay till Mrs. Eden had picked up her strength by means of rest and good plain food, provided they kept themselves quiet in the loft; and they blessed me again as if I had been their good angel.'

'It was a welcome boon, no doubt.'

'In the course of that day it came out that Mrs. Eden had not long before lost her first baby, and that she had fretted for it a good deal. This confirmed my idea that these people were instruments sent me by Providence, and I laid my plans, and arranged everything clearly in my own mind. A fortnight went by, and the snow began to melt in the valleys, and our men had hard work to keep the place from being flooded. Michael was out all day helping to cut drains to carry the water off the stackyard. As the weather brightened Mr. Eden seemed to get uneasy in his mind. "You'll be wanting to get rid of us, ma'am," he said. "The wayfarers must resume their journey through the wilderness of life." But I told him he could stay till the weather was milder, on account of his sickly wife. I was not ready for them to leave yet awhile.'

'And in all this time no one discovered them?' asked Maurice.

'No; that part of the premises lies out of every one's way. You may go and look at it to-morrow, if you like, and see what a deserted corner it is. They had a fright once or twice— heard the men's voices near, but no one ever ap- proached the loft. I took care to pay my visits to

them at meal-times, when there was no one about
to see me. I always kept my dairy under lock
and key, and I used to put the supplies for my
pensioners in the dairy. It was easy to carry things
from the dairy to the loft without being observed.
I fed them well, gave them a few old books to
read, and gave Mrs. Eden working materials, and
a piece of calico to make under-clothes for herself,
and a useful gown or two into the bargain. I had
ample stores of all kinds hoarded up, and it was
easy enough for me to be charitable.'

'Your pensioners did not grow tired of their
retreat?'

'Far from it. They had suffered too much from
actual want not to be thankful for food and shelter
which cost them nothing. Mr. Eden told me that
he had never been happier than in that loft. I had
contrived to take them over blankets, and a few old
cushions to sit upon, and many other comforts, by
degrees. Mrs. Eden's health had wonderfully improved. One day, after she had been talking to me
of the child she had lost, I asked her if she could love
and cherish a motherless infant confided to her care.

She said she could, indeed, with all her heart, and her whole face softened at the thought. It was a kind and gentle face at all times. I asked her no further questions upon the subject, but I felt full confidence in her. A week after that I took her a new-born babe in the dead of the night—a sweet little lily-faced creature dressed in the baby clothes my own fingers had stitched for my own first born child, Muriel. Heaven knows what I suffered that night when I laid the innocent lamb in Mrs. Eden's arms—she only half wakened, and scared by the suddenness of my coming. I had meant to tell her that the infant was the child of one of my servants; but when the time came I could not utter the lie. I told her only that the child was motherless, and that I confided it to her care from that hour, and that on consideration of Mr. Eden and herself taking the babe into their keeping and bringing it up as their own, I would give them a good sum of money to start them in a respectable way of life. But before I did this they must pledge themselves never again to appear at Borcel End, or anywhere in the neighbourhood of Borcel End, and never to make any application to me on account of the child. From the hour they left Borcel End the child would belong wholly to them, and there would be no link to connect it with me. I said all this hurriedly that night, but I repeated it again next day in a formal manner, and made them take a solemn oath upon my Bible, binding them to perform their part of the bond.'

'Did they stay long at Borcel after the child's birth?'

'Only five days, for I dreaded lest the baby's crying should be heard by any one about the place. Mrs. Eden took great care of the helpless little thing, and kept it wonderfully quiet, but the fear of its crying haunted me day and night. I was always fancying I heard it. I used to start up from my pillow in the dead of the night, with the sound of that child's crying in my ears, and used to wonder my husband was not awakened by it, although it would not have been possible for the sound to reach our bedroom if the child had cried its loudest. But though I knew this, the sound haunted me all the same, and I determined that the Edens should start directly it was reasonably safe for the infant to be moved. The weather was now mild and dry, the mornings were light soon after six o'clock.'

'How did you get them away secretly?'

'That was my great difficulty. There was no possibility of going away in any vehicle. They must go on foot, and make their way back to Seacomb. At Seacomb they would take the train and get out of the county. After thinking it over a long time, I decided that the safest thing would be for them to leave at half-past six o'clock in the morning, when the men would be all in the fields. I knew exactly what was going forward upon the farm, and could make my plans accordingly. It would be easy for me to take care that the maid-servant was safely employed indoors, and could see nothing of Mr. and Mrs. Eden's departure.'

'Did you give these people much money?'

'All that I possessed in the world—my secret savings of years. Good as my husband is, and well to do though we were from the beginning, it had pleased me to save a little money that was quite my own, to dispose of as I pleased, unquestioned by

Michael. I had wronged no one in saving this money, it was all the result of small economies, and of self-denial. My husband had given me a five-pound note for a new gown, and I put the money away, and turned my last silk gown instead of buying a new one, or I had reared a brood of choice poultry, and sold them to a neighbouring farmer. The money was honestly come by, and it amounted to over two hundred pounds, in notes and gold. I gave it to the Edens in a lump. "Now remember, that this is to start you in life," I said to them, finally, "and that on consideration of this you take the responsibility of this child's maintenance henceforward, and that she shall be called by your name, and as you thrive she shall thrive." This they pledged themselves to, most solemnly. Mrs. Eden seemed honestly attached to the desolate baby already, and I had no fear that it would be unkindly treated. Desperate as my necessities were, I do not think I could have entrusted that helpless infant to any one of whose kindness I had not felt confident.'

'Was the child christened when it left Borcel End?' asked Maurice.

He had a reason for thinking this question of considerable importance.

'No. I might have baptized it myself, had it been in danger of death. But the child was well enough, and seemed in a fair way to live. I told Mr. and Mrs. Eden to have it christened as soon as they had left Cornwall, and settled themselves in a new neighbourhood.'

'Did you tell them what name to call the infant?'

'No. It was to be their child henceforward. It was their business to choose its name.'

'They got safely away, I suppose?'

'Yes, they left secretly and safely, just as I had planned. I shall never forget that grey morning, in the chilly spring weather, and the last glimpse I had of those two wanderers—the woman with the child nestled to her breast, wrapped in my Muriel's blue cloak—the cloak it had been such pleasure to me to quilt when I was a young woman.'

Mrs. Trevanard sighed bitterly.

'I can remember sitting in this room at work at the beginning of my married life,' she said, dreamily, 'thinking what a grand thing it was to be married, and the mistress of a large house and a prosperous farm. I look back upon my life now—nine-and-thirty years of wedded life—and think how heavily the care of it weighs against the happiness, and what a life of toil it has been. "Heaping up riches, and ye know not who shall gather them."'

'Did you never hear any more of Mr. and Mrs. Eden, or the child?' asked Maurice, most anxious to hear all that was to be told by lips that must ere long be silent.

'From that day to this not a word. They have kept their promise. Whether they prospered or failed, I know not. They were neither of them past the prime of life, and there seemed to me no reason why they should not get on pretty well in some small trade, such as I advised them to try, beginning humbly with a part of their little capital. Heaven knows what may have become of them. The child may be dead—dead, years ago, taking that quiet rest which will soon be mine.'

'Or she may be living. She may have grown up beautiful, good, and clever ; such a grandchild as you would be proud to own.'

' I should never be proud of a nameless child,' answered Mrs. Trevanard, gloomily.

'The child you banished may not have been without a name. Forgive me if I speak plainly. Far be it from me to reproach you. I offer you sympathy and help, if help be possible. But I think you acted precipitately throughout this sad business. What if there were a secret marriage between your daughter and Captain Penwyn? Such a marriage might easily have taken place during the three weeks that your daughter was away from home, ostensibly on a visit to her late schoolmistress. Did you never question that lady?'

' It was not possible for me to do so. Miss Barlow retired from business very soon after Muriel's visit, and her school passed into the hands of strangers. She went abroad to live, and I could never find out where to communicate with her. But even if I had known where to address her, I should have feared to write, lest my letter should compromise Muriel. My one all-absorbing desire was to hide the disgrace that Providence had been pleased to inflict upon our family, doubtless as a chastisement for our pride.'

'What effect upon your daughter had the loss of her child?'

'Ah, that was terrible! After the baby's birth Muriel had a fever. It arose from no want of care or good nursing, for old Mrs. Trevanard nursed her with unceasing devotion, and there couldn't be a more skilful nurse than my mother-in-law. But Muriel missed the child, and the loss of it preyed upon her mind; and then, in her feverish delirium, she fancied I had taken the baby away and murdered it. We had a fearful time with her, old Mrs. Trevanard and I, while that delusion lasted, but by care we brought her through it all; and as the fever passed off she grew more reasonable, and understood that I had sent away the child to save her good name; but she was different in her manner to me from what she had been. She never kissed me or asked me to kiss her, or seemed to care to have me near her. I could see that my only daughter was estranged from me for ever. She clung to her grandmother, and it was as much as I could do by and by to get her to come downstairs and sit among us. I was very anxious to do this, if it was only to pacify her father, for he had been anxious and fidgety all the time she was away from us, and after the Edens had taken the baby away, I had been obliged to call in a doctor from Seacomb, just to satisfy Michael. The doctor listened to all that Mrs. Trevanard told him about Muriel, and just echoed what she said, and did neither good nor harm by his coming.'

'And your daughter resumed her place in the family?'

'She came among us, and sat by the fire, reading, or sometimes singing to little Martin, but she seemed in all things like the ghost of her former self, and it was heart-breaking to see her poor pale face. She would sit, with her melancholy eyes fixed on the burning logs, for half an hour at a time, lost in thought. You may judge how I felt towards the wretch who had worked this evil, when I saw his victim sitting there joyless and hopeless—she, who might have been so bright and glad but for him. Her father was dreadfully cut up by the change in Muriel. He would hang over her sometimes, calling her his poor faded child, and asking her what he could do to make her happy, and to bring the roses back to her cheeks; and sometimes, to please him, she would brighten up a little, and pretend to be her old glad self. But any one could see how hollow her smile was. I never said my prayers, night or morning, without praying God to avenge my daughter's great wrongs, and it never seemed to me that such a prayer was sinful.'

'Did your daughter ask you what had become of her child?'

'I saved her the pain of asking that question. As soon as reason returned, after the fever, I told her that the child was in safe hands, with kind people, and would be well cared for, and that she need give- herself no anxiety about its fate. "Let that dark interval in your life be forgotten, Muriel," I said, "and may God forgive you as freely as I do now." She made no answer, except to bow her head gently, as if in assent.'

'How was it that her mind again gave way, after this recovery?'

'I am coming to that presently. That was the heaviest blow of all. Just when I was beginning to hope time would work her cure, just when I fancied I could see a glimmer of the old smile brightening her pale face now and then, the blow fell. We were sitting round this hearth one evening, Muriel and her grandmother, and little Martin and I, when Michael came in, looking very much agitated. We asked him what was the matter. "The saddest thing I have heard of for many a year," he answered. "Well, we've all got our troubles! There's been bad news for the Squire up at Penwyn." Muriel started up with a faint cry, but I caught hold of her, and squeezed her hand tight, to warn her against saying anything that might betray her. "Dreadful news," Michael went on ; "Captain George, the eldest son, the one we know so well, has been murdered by the savages. Lord only knows what those red devils did to him. Scalped him, they say, tied him to a tree, and tortured him——" Muriel gave one long piercing scream, and dropped upon the stone floor. We lifted her up and carried her to bed, and the doctor was sent for post haste. I was sore afraid she would let out her secret, in her father's hearing or the doctor's, when she came round out of that death-like swoon ; but I need not have feared. Her mind was quite gone, and all her talk was mere disjointed raving. From that day to this she has been the helpless, hopeless creature you have seen her. We have kept her out of a madhouse by keeping her close, under old Mrs. Trevanard's care. We have done all we could think of to soften the misery of her state, but she has never, for the briefest interval, recovered her reason. And now I have told you all, Mr. Clissold—without reserve, confessing the wrong I have done as freely as when I acknowledge my sins to my God.'

The sick woman sank back upon the pillows, pale to the lips. That indomitable strength of will, which had been ever the distinguishing mark of her character, had sustained her throughout this prolonged effort. And deeply as he compassionated the sufferer's state, Maurice felt that it was vital to obtain from her at once, and without delay, all the information she could give him.

'I am grateful to you for having honoured me with your confidence, Mrs. Trevanard,' he said, kindly, 'and now that you have so fully trusted me, receive once more my solemn promise to do all that may lie in my power to obtain justice for your daughter, and your daughter's child. I am inclined to think that Captain Penwyn may have been less base than you believe him, and that his unhappy death alone may have prevented his making some atonement, or revealing the fact of a secret marriage between himself and your daughter. I can hardly think that a girl brought up as your daughter was brought up could be so easy a victim as you imagine her to have been. My endeavour shall be to ascertain the truth upon this point of marriage or no marriage. A young London clergyman, a friend of mine, has told me many a curious fact connected with private marriages—stray leaves of family history,—and I see no reason why this Captain Penwyn, who impressed you as an honourable and a well-meaning man, should not have contracted such a union with your daughter.'

'God grant that it was so,' ejaculated Mrs. Trevanard. 'I should go down to my grave with an easier mind if I could believe George Penwyn something less of a villain than I have considered him

for the last twenty years. When I heard of his
dreadful death in the Canadian forest, I said to
myself, "The Almighty Avenger of all wrongs has
heard my prayer!"'

'It shall also be my endeavour to find your
granddaughter,' said Maurice. 'I have a curious
fancy upon that point, but perhaps a foolish fancy,
and therefore hardly worth speaking about.'

'Pray tell me what it is.'

'It is really too foolish, and might only mis-
lead you. All I ask is that you will give me
any detail which may help me in my attempt to
discover the girl you entrusted to Mr. and Mrs.
Eden. What kind of man was this Mr Eden, for
instance?'

The sound of wheels rolling towards the
door prevented this question being answered. In
another moment the dog-cart drew up before the
porch, father and son alighted, and came into the
room, bringing a gust of fresh moorland air along
with them. The opportunity of obtaining further
detail from Mrs. Trevanard was gone for the time
being; and it might be long before Maurice again

found himself alone with her, or found her inclined to speak. He heartily wished that the attractions of Seacomb market, or of the homely hostelry where the farmers eat their substantial two o'clock dinner, had detained Michael Trevanard and his son just a little longer.

The invalid was more cheerful that evening than she had been for a long time, and something of the old air of domestic comfort seemed to return to the homestead parlour, as Maurice and the family sat at tea. Both her husband and son noticed the improvement.

'You must be rare good company,' said the farmer, 'for Bridget looks ever so much brighter for spending the afternoon with you.—Cheer up! old lady, we may cheat the doctors after all,' he added, bending over his wife affectionately as he handed her a cup of tea, the only kind of refreshment she now enjoyed.

'The doctors may have their own way about me, Michael,' answered Mrs. Trevanard, 'if I can only go down to my grave with my mind pretty easy.'

Her son drew his chair beside hers after tea,

and sat with his hand in hers, clinging to her with melancholy fondness, sadly expectant of the coming day when there would be nothing on this earth more distant from him than that motherly hand.

Maurice Clissold had pledged himself to spend the next day at Penwyn, where there was to be a cottager's flower show, in which Mrs. Penwyn and Miss Bellingham were deeply interested. It was the Squire's wife who had organized the annual exhibition, and stimulated the love of floriculture in the peasant mind by the offer of various useful and attractive prizes—a silver watch, a handsome rosewood tea-caddy, a delf dinner service, a copper tea-kettle—prizes which were dear to the tastes of the competing floriculturists, and which were eagerly competed for. The most gigantic yellow roses, the longest and greenest cucumbers, the finest bunches of grapes, the most mathematically correct dahlias were produced within a ten-mile radius of Penwyn; and by this simple means the cottage gardens and flower-pots in latticed casements which Mrs. Penwyn beheld in her walks and drives were things of beauty, and a perennial source of joy.

The show was held in a vast circular marquee erected in the grounds of the Manor House. Lady Cheshunt was one of the lady adjudicators, and sat in state, gorgeously attired in a tea-leaf coloured silk, fearfully and wonderfully made, by a Regent Street dressmaker, who tyrannized over her customers, and seemed to gratify a malicious disposition by inflicting hideous combinations of form and colour upon her too submissive patronesses.

' I really can't say I think it pretty, dear Lady Cheshunt,' said Madge, when her friend asked her opinion of this tea-leaf coloured abomination.

' No more do I, my love,' replied the dowager, calmly, ' but it's strikingly ugly. All your county people will be blazing in what they call pretty colours. This dirty greenish brown is *chic !* '

After the cottage flower-show came a German Tea for the gentlefolks, and croquet, and archery, and the usual amount of indiscriminate flirtation which accompanies those sports. Maurice found himself amongst pleasant sunshiny people, and almost enjoyed himself, which seemed, in some-wise, treason against Justina.

But even in those piney glades, while the click of the croquet balls was sounding to an accompaniment of silvery laughter, his fancy went back to the Bloomsbury parlour and the happy hours he had wasted there, and he longed to sit in his old corner reading Victor Hugo, or sipping tea out of the dragon china.

It was late when he drove back to Borcel in Michael Trevanard's dog-cart, which had been placed at his disposal for the day. When he came down to breakfast next morning, Mrs. Trevanard's chair was empty. This startled him, for, ill as she was, she had been rigidly regular in her habits, coming downstairs at eight o'clock every morning, and only retiring when the rest of the family went to bed.

On questioning Mr. Trevanard, he heard that the invalid was much weaker this morning. She had not been able to rise.

' It's a bad sign when Bridget gives **way**,' added **Michael**, despondently. 'She's not **one to** knock **under while** she has **strength to bear up** against her weakness.'

The next day and the next **the** chair remained **empty**. Maurice hung about **the** farm, hardly **knowing what to** do with himself in this time **of** trouble, **yet nowise** willing **to** desert his post. **On the third day he was summoned** to Mrs. **Trevanard's room**. Phœbe, the housemaid, came **in** quest of **him to** an **old orchard, where** he **was** fond **of** smoking his cigar.

' Missus **is very bad**, sir, **and I** believe **she's asked to see you**,' said the **girl**, breathless.

Maurice hurried **to** the house, and **to** Mrs. Trevanard's **room**. Husband and son were **standing** near the **bed**, and the **dying woman lay with** her hand clasped **in Martin's**, her eyes looking with **a strangely eager** expression **towards** the door.

At the sight of Maurice **her** wan face **brightened ever so little, and she gave a faint** choking cry.

' Want—tell you—something,' **she** gasped, half inarticulately

He went close to the bed and leaned over her.

'Dear Mrs. Trevanard, I am listening.'

'A Bible—gave—family Bible.'

That was all. She spoke no more after this; and before nightfall the windows were darkened at Borcel End, and the careful housewife had gone to that land where there is no thought of sordid things.

CHAPTER II.

WHAT was it that Mrs. Trevanard would have told
when death sealed her lips for ever ? This was the
question which Maurice Clissold asked himself many
a time in those dismal days at Borcel End, when the
house was darkened, while he and Martin sat together
in friendly silence, full of sympathy, and for the most
part alone, Mr. Trevanard preferring the solitude of
the best parlour in this day of affliction. What was
that circumstance or detail which she would have
told him, and what clue to the mystery was he to
discover from those two words, ' family Bible,' the
only words that he had been able clearly to gather
from the dying woman's disjointed speech ?

He suffered Martin to give full sway to his grief;
staunch in friendship, prompt with sympathy, but
never attempting to strangle sorrow with set speeches

of consolation ; and then one evening, when Michael
Trevanard had gone to bed, worn out with grief, and
when Martin was more composed and resigned than
he had been since his mother's death, Maurice approached the subject which absorbed all his thoughts
just now. He had told Martin that Mrs. Trevanard
had given him her confidence, but he had also told
him that the circumstances she had confided to him
must remain a profound secret.

' She has entrusted me with a hidden page of
your family history, Martin,' he said. ' If ever I
can set right the wrong that has been done—not by
your mother, she may have been mistaken in her
course of action, but she has deliberately wronged no
one—you shall know all; but if I fail, the secret
must remain a secret to the end of my life.'

' How good you are!' said Martin. 'Can I ever be
grateful enough for your interest in our troubles ? '

' My dear Martin, there is less cause for gratitude
than you imagine. I have a reason of my own for
being eager in this matter—a foolish reason, perhaps,
and most certainly a selfish one. So let there be no
talk of gratitude on your part.

This evening, finding Martin in a more comfortable frame of mind, Maurice deemed it safe to question him.

'You heard what your poor mother said to me on her death-bed?' he began.

'Every word. She was wandering, I think, poor dear soul!'

'I hardly think that, Martin. There was so much expression in her face as she looked at me, and she seemed so eager to tell me something. I feel sure that there was some additional circumstance, some previously forgotten detail of the story she had told me which she wanted to communicate in that last hour—something relating to a family Bible. Will you let me see your family Bible Martin?'

'Certainly. It is kept where all the world can see it—all the world of Borcel End, at least. It is on the side table in the best parlour. My poor father was reading it this afternoon. I'll go and get it.'

Martin took one of the candles and went into the next room, whence he speedily returned, carrying a substantial folio bound in brown leather.

This was the family Bible—a goodly volume, profusely garnished with old-fashioned woodcuts, and printed in a large fat-faced type on thick ribbed paper, mellowed to a yellowish hue by the passage of years.

On the fly-leaf were recorded the births, marriages, and deaths of the Trevanards for the last hundred and fifty years, but beyond this plain straightforward catalogue the page held nothing. There was the first inscription, in ink of a faded brownish hue, recording the marriage of Stephen Trevanard of Treworgy, with Justina Penrose, of St. Austell, July 14, 1773, a marriage from which the Borcel End branch of the Trevanards had arisen; and the last entry, in Michael Trevanard's sprawling penmanship, recording the death of Bridget, the beloved wife, &c., &c. Maurice read every line of that family catalogue—Muriel's birth, Martin's, but there was nothing here to suggest the faintest clue to Mrs. Trevanard's dying words.

Then carefully, and leaf by leaf, he went through the volume, looking for any stray document which might lurk between the pages. Here he found a

withered flower, with its faint ghost-like odour of departed sweetness, there a scrap of sacred poetry copied
in a girlish hand—such a pretty graceful penmanship,
which he surmised to be Muriel's.   Yes, here was one
half-sheet of note-paper, with **an extract from Milton's
Hymn, signed** 'Muriel Trevanard, Christmas, 1851.'

'May I keep this scrap of paper, Martin?' he
asked.

It struck him that it might at some future time
be well for him to **possess a specimen** of Muriel
Trevanard's writing—ready **to be** compared with any
other document.

'**By all** means,' answered Martin. 'Poor girl!
She used **to** be **so** fond of poetry.   Many **a** quaint
old Scottish **ballad has** she repeated to me, learned
out of **some** old books my father had picked up for
her at a stall in Seacomb market.'

Beyond those loose leaves of manuscript poetry,
and those stray flowerets, **Maurice's most careful
search** could discover nothing between **the** pages
of the family Bible.   He **began to** think **that**
Martin **was** right, and that those last words of
Mrs. Trevanard were but the meaningless babble

of a mind astray; with no more significance than Falstaff's dying talk of fair green fields familiar to his boyhood, or ever he had learned to find pleasure in midnight carouses, or the company of Mistress Tearsheet.

'By-the-bye,' said Martin suddenly, while his friend sat with his arms folded on the sacred volume, deep in thought, 'there's a Bible somewhere that belonged to my great-grandmother—a Bible I can just remember when I was a little chap—before Muriel's wits went astray, a Bible with queer old pictures in it, which I was very fond of looking at; not a big folio like this, but a thick dumpy volume, bound in black leather, with a brass clasp. My mother generally used it when she read the Scriptures of a Sunday evening, and it was called Mother's Bible.'

'Was there anything written in it?' asked Maurice.

'Yes, there was writing upon the first page, I believe.'

'How long is it since you saw that Bible, Martin?'

'How long?' echoed Martin, meditatively 'Oh,

ever so many years. Why, I don't remember having seen that book since I was quite a little lad.'

'Did you ever see it after your sister's mind went wrong ? '

'That's asking too much. I can't remember so closely as that ; and yet, on reflection, I don't think I ever did see it after Muriel's long illness. I was sent to Helston Grammar School just at that time, and I certainly don't remember ever having seen that Bible after I went to school. However, I dare say it's somewhere about the house. Nothing is ever lost at Borcel. That Bible is among my poor mother's stores, most likely. She was always a great hand for keeping old things.'

' I should like very much to see it, if you could find it for me by and by, Martin.'

By and by meant when that solemn presence of the dead, which set its seal upon all things at Borcel, had been removed from the old farmhouse.

' I'll look for it among mother's books next week,' said Martin. ' There are a good many books upon the old walnut-wood chest of drawers in her bedroom.'

*   *   *   *   *

Maurice stayed at Borcel all through that dismal
week, though he received a very kind letter from
Mrs. Penwyn, begging him to take up his abode at
the Manor House for the rest of his stay in Cornwall.
He felt that it would be a hard thing to leave Martin
in that house of gloom, and he knew that his presence there was some kind of comfort, even to
Michael Trevanard, who had given way to complete
despondency since his wife's death. The look of the
place was so strange to him without Bridget, he com-
plained. For nine-and-thirty years she had been the
chief person in that house—the prop and stay of all
things—the axis upon which the wheel of life
turned. The farmer knew that he owed her the
maintenance and increase of his fortune. It was
Bridget's help, Bridget's indefatigable spirit guiding
and sustaining him, which had made him rich enough
to buy Borcel, had the Squire been disposed to sell
it. She had taught him to hoard his money—she
had held him back from all share in the boisterous
pleasures of his class; but she had kept his table
liberally, provided assiduously for all his creature
comforts; and, in a drowsy monotonous way, had

made life very easy to him. He looked round him now, and seeing her vacant chair, wondered what he was to do with the remnant of his days.

The silent horror of the house stupefied him. He went in and out of the rooms in a purposeless manner; he looked into the kitchen where the two girls sat stitching away at their black gowns, and looking forward to the funeral as a ceremonial in which it was rather a grand thing to be concerned. He went into old Mrs. Trevanard's bedroom, to which apartment the old lady was still confined by that chronic rheumatic gout which at times crippled her.

Here he sat himself down by the fireside, drearily, with his elbows on his knees, looking at the fire, silent for the most of his time, and shaking his head despondently when his mother essayed some feeble attempt at consolation—some Scriptural phrase, which had been aired at all the deaths in the family for the last sixty years.

'I never thought that she would have gone before me,' crooned the old lady, 'but the Lord's ways are wonderful, and His paths past finding out. It's a sad thing to think that Muriel can't follow to-morrow. It will be the first time in our family that a daughter has been absent at her mother's funeral.'

'Ah! poor Muriel,' said the father, hopelessly. '*That* trouble seems harder to bear now. It would have comforted me in my loss if I had had a daughter to take my dead wife's place; some one to look after the servants and pour my tea out of a morning; some one to sit opposite me at table, and help me off with my coat when I came in of a wet evening.'

'There's Martin,' said old Mrs. Trevanard, 'he ought to be a comfort to you.'

'Martin's a good fellow, but he can't be what a daughter might have been. A daughter would put her arms round my neck, and cling to me, and shed her tears upon my breast; and in trying to comfort her I should almost forget my own sorrow. A daughter could fill her mother's empty place in the house, which Martin can never do. He'll be wanting to run away from home, fast enough, you'll see, now his mother's gone. She had a great deal more influence over him than I ever had. Who hadn't she influence over, I wonder? Why, the very cowboys thought more of her than of **me.**   Ah, she **was** a wonderful woman!'

'Yes, Michael,' answered his mother, **with a sigh.** 'She was a good and faithful servant, and in such the Lord is well **pleased.**   She **never** missed morning and afternoon **service, let** the weather be what it might on **Sundays.**   She read her Bible diligently, and she **did her duty to** the best of her knowledge. If ever she was mistaken——'

'She never was mistaken,' interrupted the widower, testily; 'Bridget was always right.   When Martin bought those Kerry cows, and **I** scolded him for buying **such** small mean-looking cattle, Bridget stood by him and said she'd warrant they were good milch **cows.**   **And so** they **were.**   **I** never knew Bridget out of her reckoning.'

The grandmother sighed.   **She** had been thinking of something wide apart **from the sordid cares of** farm or homestead.

Maurice attended the funeral, which took place **on a** chilly September afternoon, when autumn's biting blast swept across the broad moorland, and over the quiet valleys, and stripped the yellowing leaves from the orchard trees. The leaves were falling earlier than usual this year, after the long droughts and heat of the summer.

There were three mourning coaches, in the first of which Michael Trevanard and his son sat in solemn state. The second was occupied by Maurice, the doctor, and a neighbouring farmer; the third by three other farmers, long-standing acquaintances of the Borcel End family. These people and their households had constituted Mrs. Trevanard's world. It was for the maintenance of her respectability in their eyes she had toiled and striven; to be deemed wealthy, and honourable, and upright above all other women of her class had been her desire, and she had been gratified. They followed her to the little churchyard on the brown hill-side, discoursing of her virtues as they went, and declaring her the paragon of wives.

They laid her in the family grave of the Trevanards, and left her there just as the sun declined, and an air of evening solitude crept over the scene. And then they went back to Borcel End, where the blinds were all drawn up, and the house had put on a factitious aspect of cheerfulness. The table was plenteously spread with sirloin and chine, fowls and ham, decanters of port and sherry, shining tea-tray and silver teapot, all the best things in the house brought out to do honour to Mrs. Trevanard's obsequies. The four farmers and the doctor sat down to this feast with appetites sharpened by the autumn breezes, and poor Michael took his place at the head of the table, and did his best to perform the duties of hospitality; and the funeral guests enjoyed themselves not a little during the next hour or so, though they studiously preserved the solemnity of their countenances, and threw in a sigh now and then, midway between fowl and ham, or murmured some pious commonplace upon the brevity of life, as they held their plates for a second slice of beef.

'Ah,' said the fattest and wealthiest of the farmers, 'she was a respectable woman. There's not her equal within twenty miles of Seacomb.'

And this was the praise for which Mrs. Trevanard had toiled—this was the highest honour she had ever desired.

CHAPTER III.

FIRE THAT IS CLOSEST KEPT BURNS MOST OF ALL.

MAURICE did not leave Borcel End for some days
after the funeral. He saw how Martin clung to him
in this dark hour, when the sense of bereavement
was still a new and strange pain to the young heart,
and, anxious though he was to return to his library
and Justina, he lingered, loth to leave, since departure might seem unkind. When he told Martin
that he had literary work to do—that young man
being aware that his friend was some manner of
author, though not in the least suspecting him to be
capable of poetry—Martin argued that it was just
as easy to write at Borcel End as in London; easier,
indeed, since there was so small a chance of
interruption.'

'I've heard you say that the great beauty of
your trade is, that it requires no "plant," except,

a ream of paper and a bundle of pens,' said Martin.

'Did I say that? Ah, I forgot one important item—the library of the British Museum, some millions of books, more or less; I may not want to refer to them very often, perhaps, but I like to have them at my elbow.'

'The book you're writing is something prodigiously learned, then, I conclude,' said Martin.

'Not at all, but it is nice to be able to verify a quotation. But I'll tell you what I'll do with you, Martin. I'll stop at Borcel a week, if you'll promise to go to London with me when I leave. You told me that your poor mother's death would set you free.'

'So it will by and by; but not just yet. It would be unkind to leave father while his grief is fresh. He's so completely down.'

'Upon my word, Martin, I'm afraid you're right,' answered Maurice. 'But, remember, you must come to me directly you feel at liberty to leave Borcel—come to me and share my home, just as you would if I were your elder brother.'

Martin employed the day after the funeral in looking over his dead mother's hoards, a painful task, but not a difficult one. Bridget Trevanard's possessions had been kept with the most perfect neatness, every scrap of lace or ribbon folded and laid in its place. All the old-fashioned trinkets of her girlhood treasured in their various boxes ; the desk and workbox of her school days in perfect order. Strange that these trifles should be so much less perishable than their owner.

But despite his careful examination of his mother's drawers and boxes, Martin failed to find the object of his search, that old family Bible with the clasps, which he had described to Maurice. The book was nowhere to be found. Martin distributed his mother's clothes, the best to old Mrs. Trevanard, to do what she liked with, the rest to the two handmaidens, both tolerably faithful after their manner, and honestly regretful of a mistress who, though sharp and exacting, had been just in her dealings with them, and careful of their comfort. The trinkets, and workbox, and desk, and little collection of gift-books, chiefly of a devotional character, Martin Trevanard put away, under lock and key, in the old bureau, opposite his mother's bed. He kept them for Muriel, with the faint idea that some day the light of reason might return, if only in some small measure, to that clouded brain.

'No one else has so good a right to them,' he said to himself, as he put away these homely treasures, 'and no one else shall have them while I live.'

'I suppose my dear mother must have given that Bible away,' he said to Maurice, after describing his unsuccessful search. 'And yet it was hardly like her to give away an old family Bible. She was one who set so much store by old things, and above all by her religious books.'

At that moment there flashed across Maurice's recollection one hitherto forgotten word in the dying woman's broken sentence.

'Gave—family Bible—'

That word 'gave' confirmed Martin's idea. The Bible had been given away—but to whom? and why did it concern Maurice, in his endeavour to right the wrongs of the past, to know that fact?

Why, indeed, unless the Bible had been given to Mr. and Mrs. Eden, the people who took Muriel's infant?

He went over in his note-book the story which Bridget Trevanard had told him. He had been careful to write down all the facts, recording every detail as closely as possible, a few hours after he received that story of the past from the invalid's lips. Going over it carefully in the silence of his own room on the second night after the funeral, he came to this passage—'I made them take a solemn oath upon my Bible, binding them to perform their part of the bond.'

It was clear, then, that Mrs. Trevanard had carried her Bible to the loft—that the oath had been sworn upon her own Bible. Was it not likely that on so solemn an occasion as her parting with these people, who were to carry the last of her race —the nameless child she discarded—away with them, she, a woman of deep religious convictions, might have given them her Bible, the most sacred gift she could bestow, symbol of good faith between them ?

Now if this Bible had been given, and the name of Martin's great-grandmother, Justina Trevanard, was written in it, the fact would add one more link to that chain of evidence which Maurice Clissold had been putting together lately.

It had entered into his mind that Justina Elgood was Muriel's daughter—the child given into the keeping of strangers, perhaps—ah! too bitter thought, the child of shame.

The facts in support of this notion were not many, would have made very little impression, perhaps, in a court of justice, yet, though he struggled against a notion which appeared to his sober reason absurd and groundless, his fancy was taken captive, and dwelt upon the idea with a tormenting persistence.

In the first place he was a poet, and there seemed to him a curious fatality in all the circumstances connected with his presence at Borcel End. He had gone there by the merest accident, guided by that will-o'-the-wisp of a child, tramping miles across a barren moor, intruding himself on an unwilling hostess. Then on the very first night of his habitation beneath that lonely roof he had been visited by one who, if not a wanderer from the shadow-world, was at least a ghost of the past; one who had outlived life's joys and hopes, almost its cares and sorrows. This appearance of Muriel's had at once awakened his interest in her. But for this midnight visit, and the chance meeting in the hazel copse, he might have come and gone a dozen times without being aware of Muriel Trevanard's existence.

This idea of Destiny was, of course, a mere fanciful reason.

To-night in the silence, having gone over every word of Mrs. Trevanard's story in his note-book, he placed on record those other circumstances which had impressed him in relation to this question.

1. The fact that Justina Elgood was said to have been born at Seacomb, a curiously out-of-the-way corner of the earth.

2. Her age exactly corresponded with the age of Muriel's daughter, were she living.

3. The particularly uncommon name of Justina, a family name of the Trevanards.

4. The description of the man who had called him-
    self Eden ; a fluent speaker, a man who
    seemed accustomed to public speaking.

5. Matthew Elgood had lost an infant daughter
    at Seacomb.   The fact stood recorded in the
    register.   These Edens had also lost a child.

Very little certainly, all this, when set down
formally upon paper, but the idea floating in
Maurice's mind seemed to have a stronger founda-
tion than these meagre facts.   Whence the fancy
came he knew not, yet it seemed to him that for
a long time he had been sceptical as to Justina's
relationship to Matthew Elgood.   There was so
evident a superiority in the daughter to the supposed father.   They were creatures of a different
clay.

‘ It is just as if some clumsy delf pitcher were
to pretend to be made of the same paste as Justina's
dragon china tea service,’ he said to himself.

He remembered how reticent Mr. Elgood had
always been upon the subject of the past—how the
little that he had even told had been told somewhat
reluctantly, extorted, in a manner, by Maurice's

questioning. He remembered Mr. Elgood's startled look when he, Maurice, had spoken for the first time of Borcel End.

'I dare say, after all, the fancy is groundless,' he said to himself, as he closed his pocket-book, 'and that the circumstances which have impressed me so strongly could be explained in quite a different manner. A provincial actor's wandering life may bring him to any corner of the earth' and the name Justina may have been chosen out of some novel of the day by Mrs. Elgood. But since I have promised to do my uttermost to see Muriel Trevanard righted, I am bound to sift this matter thoroughly. And again, it would be hard if I were not allowed to investigate the pedigree of the woman I hope to win for my wife. The worst or the best that I can learn of my darling's parentage will make no difference in my love for her true self.'

For three or four days after the funeral Maurice gave himself up almost entirely to friendship, and spent his time strolling about the farm with Martin, philosophizing, consoling, talking hopefully of the future, when the young man was to come to London, and carve out some kind of career for himself. But the last two days of his stay in Cornwall Mr. Clissold had apportioned to his own business. One day for a farewell visit to Penwyn Manor, another day for Seacomb, where he had certain inquiries and researches to make. He had arranged to leave Borcel the morning after his visit to the Manor House, and to spend the following night at an hotel in Seacomb. This would give him the whole of the day and evening in that somewhat melancholy town.

He had written to Mrs. Penwyn, gratefully acknowledging her kind invitation to make the Manor House his head-quarters, and explaining that his friendship for Martin obliged him to decline her hospitality. But in his heart of hearts there was another reason why he did not care to stay at Penwyn Manor, or increase his intimacy with Churchill Penwyn. Justina had expressed her antipathy to that gentleman, and Maurice felt as if it were in some manner treasonable to cultivate the friendship of any man whom Justina disliked. That large madness, Love, is a conglomeration of small follies.

Courtesy, however, demanded that he should pay his respects to the Penwyn family before leaving Cornwall, and he had a lurking curiosity about that household—a somewhat morbid interest, perhaps, with which Justina's vague suspicions, far as they were from any thought of his own, may have had something to do.

That change in Madge Penwyn—hardly to be described, yet, to his eye, very palpable—had puzzled him not a little. Was it possible that the husband and wife, so devoted to each other a little while ago, had undergone some change of feeling? that one or the other had looked back upon the sunlit path of love, and perceived that the rose-bloom was fading from life's garden? No, Maurice could not for a moment believe in any lessening of Madge Penwyn's love of her husband, or Churchill's devotion to her. He had seen that 'little look across the crowd' which the poet has sung of—the look of utter trust and sympathy which passes between a husband and wife now and then in some busy hour of the day, amidst some friendly circle, a sudden interchange of thought or feeling, stolen from the throng. And in Madge's case he had seen a look of devotion curiously pathetic, love fraught with pity—a look of deepest melancholy. This dwelt in his memory, and influenced his thoughts of Churchill Penwyn and his wife. There was some hitch; some dissonant interval in the harmony of their lives; yet what the jarring notes could be it was hard for the student of humanity to discover. No life could seem outwardly more perfect. Churchill's position was of all positions most enviable. Just sufficient wealth for all the joys of life ; an estate large enough to give him importance in his neighbourhood, without the weighty responsibility of a large landowner ambition gratified by his parliamentary success ; the fairest wife that man could desire to adorn his home. And yet there were shadows on the face of husband and wife that denoted a secret trouble. In this house which held all things the skeleton was no t wanting.

'Can there be any ground for Justina's suspicion?' Maurice asked himself. 'And is a clear conscience the one thing, missing in Churchill Penwyn's sum of happiness?'

CHAPTER IV.

It was a dull autumnal afternoon when Maurice paid his final visit to the Manor House. That brilliant summer, which had lasted in all its heat and glory to the end of August, and even extended to September, had vanished all at once, and had given place to a bleak and early autumn. Stormy winds by night, and dull grey skies by day, had prevailed of late ; sad stories of disaster at sea filled many a column in the newspapers—to the relief of editors, who must needs have had recourse to gigantic gooseberries, or revivified the sea-serpent, but for these catastrophes.

Even the Manor House had a gloomy look under this leaden sky. Pyramids of scarlet geraniums, thickets of many-coloured dahlias, lent their gaudy hues to the scene ; but the lack of sunlight made all dull. The gilded vane pointed persistently north-east.   Gardeners and underlings had laboured in vain to keep the paths and lawns clear of dead leaves. Down they came, in a crackling shower, with every gust, emblems of decay and death. Maurice Clissold, sensitive, as the poet must ever be, to external influences, felt depressed by the altered aspect of the place.

Within, however, all was mirth and brightness. There was the usual family group in the hall, where a mighty wood fire blazed in the antique grate, with its massive ironwork, and two burnished brazen globes, on iron standards—golden orbs that reflected the ruddy glow of the fire. The billiard-players were at work. A party of young ladies playing pool industriously, under the leadership of Mr. Tresillian, J. P., who was in great force in feminine circles where there was not much strain upon a man's intellect. Lady Ches-hunt was in her pet chair by the fire—her com-plexion guarded by a tapestry banner-screen—deeply absorbed in that very French novel the iniquity whereof she had seen denounced by the critical journals. Viola Bellingham was working point-lace

at a little table by the central window, and listening
with rather a listless air to Sir Lewis Dallas's dis-
course.   Neither Madge nor her husband was
present.

Lady Cheshunt closed her novel with a faint
sigh, leaving a finger between the pages. Mr. Clissold
was not so interesting as the last and worst of
French novelists; yet she felt called upon to be
civil to him.

'How is Mrs. Penwyn?' he asked, when he had
shaken hands with, and duly informed himself as to
the health of, the distinguished dowager.

'That poor child is not very well,' replied her
ladyship. 'East wind, I suppose. I don't think we
were created for a world in which the wind is perpetually in the east. On such a day as this I always
wish myself in the torrid zone, the centre of Africa,
anywhere where one could feel the sun.   To look at
that grey sky and those falling leaves is enough to
give one the horrors. It's as bad as reading Young's
"Night Thoughts," or staying at a country house
with goody-people, who insist upon reading one of
Blair's sermons aloud on a wet Sunday afternoon.'

'I hope it is nothing serious,' said Maurice, meaning Mrs. Penwyn's indisposition.

'Oh dear no, not in the least. She is only a little out of spirits, and has been spending the morning in her own room with the baby. I dare say she will come down presently. I think she worked a little too hard last season, giving dinners to all the people Mr. Penwyn wanted to conciliate, and going everywhere he wished. She would make an admirable Cabinet minister's wife, I tell her, so devoted and self-sacrificing; and I suppose, at the rate Mr. Penwyn is going on, he is sure to be in the Cabinet sooner or later. A very wonderful man—so serious and self-contained—a man who never wasted a minute of his life, I should think.'

Madge entered at this moment, a little paler than in the days of old, but very beautiful. Her flowing grey silk dress, with broad sash and gimps and fringes of richest violet, became her admirably. Not a jewel or ornament, except the single amethyst stud which fastened her plain linen collar, and the triple band of diamonds on her wedding finger. The plenteous dark hair wound coronet fashion

round the small head.   A woman for a new Velas-
quez to paint, just as she stood before Maurice
to-day in the soft grey light.

'I am so sorry to hear you have been ill,' he said,
as they shook hands.

'But you must not be sorry, for I was not really
ill. I was a little tired, perhaps a little idle, too,
and I wanted a morning alone with my boy. What
have you done with Churchill, Lady Cheshunt?'
with a little anxious look round the room—empty
for her, lacking that one occupant.

'What have I. done with him?' ejaculated the
dowager. 'Do you suppose your husband is a man
to be kept indoors by any fascinations of mine? I
should as soon expect to see Brutus, or Cassius, or
any of those dreadful Shakesperian persons in togas,
playing the tame cat. I asked your husband to
read aloud to us, thinking that might please him—
most men are proud of their elocution,—but you
should have seen his look of quiet contempt. "I
am so sorry I am too busy to allow myself the
pleasure of amusing you," he said, and then went off
to superintend some new plantation of Norwegian
firs. Wonderful man!'

'You have come to spend the rest of the day with us of course, Mr. Clissold ?' said Madge, with that pleasant cordial manner which was one of her charms, and in no wise out of harmony with her somewhat queenly bearing. Who more delightful than a queenly woman when she desires to please?

'I shall be only too happy if I may, and if you will excuse my appearing at dinner in a frock coat. I reserved this day for my visit here. It is my last day but one in the west.'

'I am so sorry,' said Madge. 'Well, since we have you for so short a time we must do our best to amuse you. Perhaps,' with a happy thought, 'you would like to go and see Churchill's new plantation. We might go for a drive and join him.'

Maurice understood the wife's desire to be near her husband, a new proof of that love which had an element of pathos in its quiet intensity.

'I should like it of all things,' he answered.

'But are you sure you have lunched ?' It was between three and four in the afternoon.

'Quite sure. I joined Mr. Trevanard at his early dinner.'

'Clara—Laura, which of you will come for a drive?' asked Madge, indiscriminately of the pool-players. 'I know it would be useless to ask you, dear Lady Cheshunt.'

'My love, I would as soon drive across the Neva in a sledge for pleasure. I never stir from my fireside, except to go out to dinner, when the wind's in the east. Setting aside the discomfort, I can't see why one should make a horror of one's self by exposing one's complexion to be rasped as the bakers rasp their rolls.'

The pool-players were too deeply involved in their game to care about leaving it, unless dear Mrs. Penwyn particularly wished them to go out.

'Let me come, Madge,' said Viola, 'and let us take Nugent.—You won't mind, will you, Mr. Clissold?'

'Do you think that I am such a barbarian as to object to that small individual's society?' asked Maurice. 'He shall sit on my knee, and pull my beard as hard as he likes.'

Sir Lewis Dallas asked to be allowed to join the party, so the sociable was ordered, and Mrs. Penwyn and her sister retired to put on their hats.

' She is not looking well,' said Maurice.

' No, she is not,' answered Lady Cheshunt, with more earnestness than was common to that somewhat frivolous dowager. ' She has never been quite the same since that burglar business.'

' Indeed!   The alarm caused her a great shock, I suppose.'

' Well, she knew nothing about the attempt until it was all over; but I suppose the worry and excitement afterwards were too much for her. The man turned out to be a son of the lodge-keeper, and the woman came whining to Mrs. Penwyn to get him let off easily; and Madge, who is the most tender-hearted creature in the world, persuaded Churchill to use his influence with that good-natured Mr. Tresillian, whom he can wind round his finger,' in a whisper, ' and the man got off. It was particularly good of Mrs. Penwyn, for I know she detests that lodge woman.'

' Really!' said Maurice, affecting ignorance. ' Then I wonder Mr. Penwyn keeps her on his premises, now that he knows her son to be such a dangerous character.'

'Yes, it's just one of those absurd things men do for the sake of having their own way. I've talked to Mr. Penwyn about it myself ever so many times. "Why do you annoy your poor wife by keeping a horrid creature like that?" I have asked him. "Suppose I know your horrid creature to be deserving of protection and shelter, Lady Cheshunt? Should I not be unmanly if I were to sacrifice her to a foolish prejudice of Madge's?" he retorts. So both Madge and I have left off talking about the creature; but I must say that it always makes me feel uncomfortable to see her squatting on the threshold in the sunshine, like an overgrown toad.'

'Perhaps I could tell Mr. Penwyn something about his *protégée's* antecedents that would make him change his opinion.'

'Then pray do. But is it anything very dreadful?—murder, or anything of that kind?' asked Lady Cheshunt, with a scared look. 'You make me feel as if we were all going to have our throats cut.'

'It is nothing very dreadful. Perhaps hardly enough to cause any change in Mr. Penwyn' opinion.   I remember that woman plying her trade as a gipsy fortune-teller at Eborsham, the day before my poor friend, James Penwyn, was murdered. She in a manner—by the merest accident, of course—foretold James's early death.'

'Dear me, what an extraordinary thing! And you find her, two years afterwards, in Churchill Penwyn's service. That is very curious.'

'The whirligig of time brings many curious things to pass, Lady Cheshunt. But here are the ladies.'

They went to the porch, where the sociable was waiting for them with a pair of fine bays, impatient to be gone. It was not an inviting day for open-air excursions, but just one of those grey afternoons which have a kind of poetry—a sentiment all their own. The sombre expanse of moorland, dun colour against the grey, had a fine effect.

They took a longish drive, made a circuit, and came round to the new plantation, where Churchill was superintending the work, seated on his favourite, Tarpan, an animal which had of late shown himself unmanageable by any one except his master, and had been the cause of more than one groom's retirement from a service which was in every other respect admirable. Churchill seemed to have a peculiar fancy for the somewhat ill-conditioned brute, though he did not often ride him, on account of Mrs. Penwyn's apprehensions.

'My dear love, he will never throw *me*,' Churchill said, in answer to his wife's request that Tarpan should be disposed of. 'If I were not thoroughly convinced of that I would part with him. The brute understands me, and I understand him, which neither of those fellows did. And I like his pace and action better than those of any other horse in the stable. Nothing revives me like a gallop on Tarpan.'

Wonderful to see the influence of Madge Penwyn's presence on her husband, as Maurice saw it to-day. The moody brow relaxed its contemplative frown, the thoughtful eye brightened, while a gentle pressure of the hand and a fondly whispered greeting welcomed the wife.

'This is an unexpected pleasure, Madge,' he said. 'I did not think you would drive to-day.'

'I wanted to show Mr. Clissold your new plantation, Churchill.'

They all alighted, and Churchill showed them his newly planted groves, the graceful feathery Norwegian saplings, a ship-load of them brought from Norway for his special benefit, rhododendrons planted in between, and here and there a mountain ash or a copper beech to give colour and variety.

While they were walking in the plantation, Maurice and Churchill side by side, the former seized the opportunity of speaking of the gipsy woman whose presence at Penwyn Manor was a perplexity to him. It might possibly be an impertinence on his part to call in question Mr. Penwyn's domestic arrangements, but Maurice felt that there were circumstances in this case which fully justified a breach of manners.

'Do you know that I have made a curious discovery about a person in your employment, Mr. Penwyn?' he began.

'Indeed, and pray who and what is the person?' asked Churchill, with the slightest possible change of manner, from cordiality to reserve.

'Your lodgekeeper,' replied Maurice; and then he proceeded to relate the circumstances of his first meeting with Rebecca Mason.

Mr. Penwyn received the information with supreme indifference.

'Curious,' he said, carelessly, 'but I have long since discovered that life is made up of curious coincidences, and I have lost the faculty of astonishment. Multitudinous as the inhabitants of this globe are, we seem to be perpetually moving in circles, and knocking our heads against some one or other connected with our past lives. If I had wronged a man in Otaheite twenty years ago, it would not in the least surprise me to meet him at Seacomb Corn Exchange to-morrow. With regard to the woman Mason, I found her in circumstances of extreme distress, and offered her a home. It was one of those rare occasions on which I have indulged in the luxury of doing good,' with an ironical laugh. 'I knew, when I did this, that Rebecca had gipsy blood in her veins, and had led a roving life. But I had reason to believe her an honest woman then, and I have never found any cause for thinking her otherwise since. And this being so. I have made up my mind to keep her, in spite of the vulgar prejudice against her tawny skin—in spite even of my wife's dislike.'

'You are not alarmed by the idea of her relationship to a burglar?'

'No. First and foremost, I am not prepared to admit that the man is a burglar; and secondly, if he be, I am as well able to defend the Manor House from him as from any other member of his profession.'

'Except that he would have the advantage of his mother's lodge as a base of operations, and his mother's knowledge of your domestic arrangements,' remonstrated Maurice, determined to push the question.

'I have told you that I know Rebecca to be an honest woman, whatever the son may be. Come, Mr. Clissold, we may as well drop this subject. You are not likely to influence me upon a point which I have maintained against the wish of my wife.'

'So be it,' said Maurice, closing the discussion, with the conviction that there was some hidden link between the gipsy and the Squire of Penwyn : some influence stronger than philanthropy which secured the wanderer's home. The fact that it should be so, that there should be some secret alliance between the woman who had foretold James Penwyn's death and the man who had been so large a gainer by that early death, impressed him strangely. He was thoughtful and silent throughout the homeward drive ; so thoughtful and so silent as to arouse Madge Penwyn's curiosity.

'I can hardly compliment you upon being the most amusing of companions, Mr. Clissold,' she said, with a forced smile, as they approached the Manor House. 'There was a time when your conversation used to be amusing enough to enliven the dullest drive, but to-day you have been the image of gloom.'

'Black care sits behind us all, at odd times, Mrs. Penwyn,' he answered, gravely. 'Be assured I must have cause for serious thought when the charm of your presence does not put me in spirits.'

'Thanks for the compliment; but you talk rather too much like a Greek oracle,' retorted Madge, lightly, but with an uneasy look which did not escape Maurice's observation.

'There is a cloud hanging over this house,' he said to himself. 'A trouble in which husband and wife share. But it can be no such dark secret as Justina's suspicions point to, or Mrs. Penwyn would know nothing about it. No husband would reveal such guilt as *that* to his wife.'

CHAPTER V.

'FOR THOU WERT STILL THE POOR MAN'S STAY.'

DINNER at Penwyn Manor went off gaily enough. Lady Cheshunt, inspirited by various light wines, a good deal of Maraschino in the ice pudding, and a glass of Curaçoa as a corrective afterwards, was a host in herself, and talked loud enough, fast enough, recklessly enough, to keep the dullest dinner party going. Mr. Penwyn was always an excellent host, starting fresh subjects of conversation with such admirable tact that no one knew who changed the current of ideas when interest was just beginning to flag—never taking the lion's share of the talk, or drifting into monologue—listening to every one—encouraging the timid—sustaining the weak—and proving himself a living encyclopædia whenever dates, names, or facts were wanted.

The gentlemen left the dining-room about ten minutes after the ladies had quitted it, to the delight of Sir Lewis Dallas, and the secret disgust of Mr. Tresillian, who liked to prose about stable and kennel for an hour or so over his claret.

The assembly being merely a household party, people scattered themselves in a free and easy manner through the rooms, the ivory balls clicking in hall and billiard-room, as usual, a little group of ladies round the piano trying that sweet bit of Schumann's, chiefly remarkable for syncopation, and little jerky chords meandering up and down the piano, and demanding no small skill in the executant.

Maurice found himself in the deep embrasure of one of the hall windows, talking literature with Miss Bellingham, who evidently preferred his society to that of the devoted Sir Lewis.

'A good opportunity to find out a little more about George Penwyn,' thought Maurice. Miss Bellingham must be acquainted with all the traditions of the house. If I could but discover what manner of man this Captain Penwyn was, I should be better able to arrive at a just conclusion about his relations with Muriel Trevanard.'

A little later, when they were talking of libraries and book-collecting, Viola said, 'There were hardly fifty books altogether at Penwyn, I think, when my brother-in-law came into the property. The library here is entirely Churchill's collection. The old Squire and his predecessors must have been strangely deficient of literary taste. Even the few books there were had most of them belonged to Captain Penwyn, the poor young man who was killed in Canada.'

'Ah, poor fellow! I heard of his sad fate from the housekeeper here when I came to see the Manor House last summer. A tragical end like that gives a melancholy interest to a man's history, however commonplace it may be in other respects. I suppose you have heard a good deal of gossip about this George Penwyn?'

'Yes, our old housekeeper is fond of talking about him. He seems to have been a favourite with people, especially with cottagers and small tenants on the estate. I have heard old people regret that he never came to his own, even in my presence, though the speech was hardly civil to my brother-in-law. I know that by some of the people we are looked upon as intruders, on Captain Penwyn's account. He seems to have been constantly doing kindnesses.'

'And you have never heard anything against his character—that he was dissipated—wild, as the world calls it'

'Never so much as a word. On the contrary, Mrs. Darvis has often told me that he was particularly steady—that he was never known to take too much wine, or anything of that kind. In fact, she talks as if he had been a paragon.'

'Ah,' thought Maurice, 'these paragons are sometimes viler at bottom than your open profligate. Few men ever knew the human heart better than he who gave us Charles and Joseph Surface.'

'I have an inward conviction that Captain Penwyn must have been nice,' said Viola.

'Indeed! On what is that conviction based?'

'On various grounds. First, there are the praises of people who cannot flatter, since there is nothing to be gained by speaking well of the dead. Secondly, there is that shelf full of books with George Penwyn's name in them, all nice books, the choice of a man of refinement and good feeling. Thirdly, there is his portrait, and I like his face. Are those reasons strong enough, do you think?'

'Quite, for a woman! His portrait!—ah, by-the-bye, I should like to have another look at that.'

'Come and see it at once, then,' replied Viola, good-naturedly. 'It is in the little study, yonder—the old Squire's room. The books are there too.'

The study was a little room off the hall. Maurice remembered it well, though he had never entered it since Mrs. Darvis showed him George Penwyn's portrait, on his first visit to the Manor House.

Viola took a candle from the mantelshelf and led the way to the study, a room which was still used for business interviews with stewards or tenants, a second door opening into a passage communicating with the offices, and obscure backways by which such inferior beings were admitted to the squire's presence.

Maurice took the candle from Miss Bellingham's

hand and held it up before the picture over the mantelpiece. His grip tightened on the bronze candlestick, and his breath came stronger and quicker as he looked, but he said never a word.

That picture was to him stronger confirmation of his idea about Justina's parentage than all the circumstantial evidence in the word. There, in those pictured lineaments he saw the very lines of Justina's face—lines modified in her countenance, it is true, and softened to feminine beauty, but characteristics too striking to be mistaken even by a casual observer.

'Strange that the likeness did not occur to me when I saw that picture first,' he thought. 'But at that time I had only looked at Justina with the eye of indifference. I did not know her face by heart as I do now. And I remember that even then the picture struck me as like some one I knew. Memory only failed to recall the individual.'

Those dark blue-grey eyes, with their somewhat melancholy expression, were so like the eyes he had seen looking at him mournfully only three weeks ago, when Justina bade him good-bye; the eyes

which he faintly remembered looking up at him
for the first time, in the buttercup meadow near
Eborsham.   He put down the candle without a word.

'I hope you have stared long enough at that
picture,' said Viola, laughing.   'You appear to find
it remarkably interesting.'

'It is a very interesting portrait—to me.'

'Why to you, in particular?'

'Because it resembles some one very dear to me.'

'Oh, I understand,' said Viola, gently. 'Your
poor friend, James Penwyn!'

Maurice did not attempt to set her right.

'Now let us look at the books,' he said, going to
the *secretaire*, the upper shelves of which held about
thirty volumes, all well bound.   They were Valpy's
Shakespeare, Wordsworth, Coleridge, Byron, Shelley,
Keats, Hood, and a few other volumes, chiefly Oxford
classics, which Mr. Penwyn had brought from the
University; not by any means the books of a man
wanting in refinement or culture.   That they had
been well read was evident to Maurice, on looking
into some of the volumes.   Many a verse underlined
in pencil marked the reader's appreciation.

In a volume of Byron, containing 'Manfred,' and some of the minor poems, Maurice found a pencilled note here and there, in a woman's hand, which he recognised as Muriel Trevanard's; words of praise or of criticism, but in all cases denoting a cultivated mind and a sound judgment. A girl who could write thus was hardly likely to have been fooled by the first seducer who came across her path.

'I wonder who wrote in that book?' said Viola. 'George Penwyn had no sister, and his mother died while he was very young. Perhaps those notes were written by Miss Morgrave, the young lady his father wanted him to marry.'

'I should hardly have thought they were on intimate terms enough for that kind of thing.'

'True. One must be very sure of a person's friendship before one can venture to scribble one's opinions in their books,' returned Viola.

An hour later Maurice left the Manor House. He was glad to be alone, and free to think over the day's work.

The idea which had hitherto seemed little better than a baseless fancy, the filmy weaving of his own

romantic dreams, was now conviction. He held it as
a certain fact that Justina was George Penwyn's
daughter, and that it must be his work to discover
the missing link in Muriel Trevanard's story, and
the nature of that fatal union which had ended in
shattered wits and a broken heart.

'God grant that I may find evidence to confirm
my own belief in the girl's purity and the man's
honour,' he said to himelf, as he drove the dog-cart '
back to Borcel End. 'If the popular idea of George
Penwyn is correct, he must have been too good a
man to play so base a part as that of betrayer ;
too kind to leave his victim to face the storm of
parental wrath unprotected. But he was in his
father's power, and it is possible that he might have
had recourse to a secret marriage rather than forfeit
the old man's favour and the Penwyn estate. Yet
if this were the case, it is strange that he should
have left England without endeavouring to secure
his wife's safety—that he should have made no
provision for his child's birth—an event the possibility of which he ought to have foreseen.'

This was a puzzling point. Indeed, the whole

story was involved in mystery. Either George Penwyn must have deceived everybody who knew him as to his moral character; or he must have acted honestly towards Muriel.

'There is only one person I can think of as likely to know the truth of the story,' Maurice said to himself, 'and that person is Miss Barlow, the schoolmistress at Seacomb. My first endeavour must be to find Miss Barlow, if she is still an inhabitant of this lower world.'

He had a good deal to do in Seacomb, yet was anxious, with a lover's foolish yearning, to get back to London; so he got Martin to drive him over to the quiet old market town early next morning, and took care to put up at the oldest inn in the place— a rambling old house with a quadrangular yard—a relic of the good old coaching days.

'There is no better place than an old inn in which to learn the traditions of a town,' Maurice told himself. 'I dare say I shall find some ancient waiter here who remembers everything that has happened at Seacomb for the last fifty years.'

CHAPTER VI.

I FOUND HIM GARRULOUSLY GIVEN.

THE oldest inn in Seacomb was the 'New London Inn,' built upon the site of a still more ancient hostelry, but itself nearly two hundred years old. The quadrangular yard, in which the coaches were wont to stand, was now embellished with a glazed roof, and served for the assembling of farmers on market days. Here was held the corn exchange, and samples of grain were exhibited, and bargains made, amidst a lively hubbub, while the odour of roast beef and pastry pervaded the atmosphere.

Here Maurice and Martin parted, the former telling his friend that he had business to transact in Seacomb, the young Cornishman bidding his companion a reluctant farewell.

As soon as the dog-cart had driven off, Maurice strolled into the bar, called for soda and sherry, and surveyed his ground. On the other side of the shining **counter** a comfortable-looking elderly **matron, in a** black silk **gown** and a cap with rose-coloured ribbons was engaged in conversation **with a** stalwart grey-coated farmer, **who had been** admitted to the privileged sanctorum within. ' The landlady, evidently,' **thought** Maurice.

He sipped his sherry and soda, and asked if he could **be** accommodated with an airy bedroom.

' Certainly, sir. **You'd like a room on the first** floor, perhaps, overlooking the' street ?— Chambermaid, **show** Number 10.'

' I won't trouble to **look** at the room, thank **you,** ma'am. **I've no doubt it's all that's** comfortable.'

' There's not much fear about that, **sir.** I look after **my** bedrooms myself, and always **have done** so for **the last** thirty years. I go into every room in the house every morning, after the [chambermaids have done their sweeping and **dusting;** and that's neither more nor less than a housekeeper's duty, in my opinion.'

' **Just so,** ma'am. **It's a** pity that kind of housekeeping should ever go out of fashion.'

' It is indeed, sir. You intend staying for **some**

days at Seacomb, perhaps ? There are a good many objects of interest in the neighbourhood.'

'I am sorry to say that I shall have to leave to-morrow.'

'Well, good morning, Mrs. Chadwick,' said the farmer, having drained his glass, and wiped his lips with a flaming orange handkerchief.

Mrs. Chadwick opened the half-door of the bar for him to go out, and then, holding it open politely, invited Mr. Clissold to enter.

'You may as well sit down, sir, and take your soda and sherry,' she said, nothing averse from a little gossip with the stranger.

'I shall be very glad to do so,' answered Maurice. 'The fact is, I want a little friendly chat with some one who knows Seacomb, and I dare say you know pretty well as much as any one else about the town and its inhabitants.'

The landlady smiled, as with inward satisfaction.

'It's my native town, sir. I was born here, and brought up here, and educated here, and I could count the months I've spent away from Seacomb on my fingers. It isn't everybody can say as much'

'You were educated at Seacomb,' said Maurice. 'Then perhaps you may remember Miss Barlow's school for young ladies?'

'Yes, sir. I remember Miss Barlow well, but her school flourished after my schooling days, and it was above my father's station. No Seacomb trades-people ever went to Miss Barlow's. Their money might be good enough for most people, but Miss Barlow wouldn't have it. She set her face against anything under a rich farmer's daughter. She had a good deal of pride—stuckupishness some people went so far as to call it—had Miss Barlow. And a very pretty show she used to make with her young ladies at the parish church, in the west gallery, on the left of the organ.'

'Do you happen to remember the daughter of a Mr. Trevanard, of Borcel End?'

'Remember Miss Trevanard! I should think I did. She was about the prettiest girl I ever saw, and the Seacomb gentlemen would go out of their way to get a look at her. I've seen them hanging about the church door to watch Miss Barlow's young ladies come out, and heard them whisper, "That's the

belle of the school! That's Trevanard's daughter!"
I thought she'd have made a rare good match when
she left school ; but she never married, and I believe
she went a little queer in her head, or was bedridden,
or some affliction of that kind, while she was quite
young. I haven't heard anybody mention her name
for the last twenty years—not her own father
even, though he dines here every market day. That
was young Mr. Trevanard drove you here, wasn't it ?
I just caught a glimpse of him in the hall.'

'Yes, Martin and I are great friends.'

'A very nice young man he is too, and nice-
looking, but not a patch upon his sister.'

'Do you know what became of Miss Barlow
when she left Seacomb ?'

'Well, I've heard say that she went to the Continent to cultivate music. She had a fine finger for
the piano, and [took a good deal of pride in her
playing, and after she'd lived abroad some years,
studying in a conservatory—I suppose they teach
them that way on account of the climate—I heard
that she came back to England, and settled somewhere near London, and gave lessons to the nobility

and gentry, and stood very high in that way.   She
had made a nice little fortune at Seacomb before she
retired, so she had no call to work unless she liked.
But Miss Barlow wasn't the woman to be idle.   She
had a vast amount of energy.'

A musical professor, and residing in the neighbourhood of London.   It seemed to Maurice that,
knowing this much, be ought to be able to find
Miss Barlow.   There was only the question of time.

'How long is it, do you imagine, since you last
heard of this lady ?' he asked, in a purely conver-
sational tone.

'Well, I can't take upon myself to say very
particularly for a year or so.   But I think it might
be about eight or nine years since I heard Dr.
Dorlick, our organist, say that a friend of his in
London had told him Miss Barlow was residing in
the neighbourhood of the parks, and doing wonderfully well.'

'Could I see Dr. Dorlick, do you think ?' asked
Maurice eagerly.

'Dr. Dorlick is in heaven,' replied Mrs. Chadwick,
with solemnity.

'I'm sorry for that,' said Maurice, with reference to his own disappointment rather than Dr Dorlick's elevation.

He passed on to another subject, also an important one in his mind.

'How is it that you managed to do away with your theatre in Seacomb?' he asked.

'Well, you see, sir,' returned Mrs. Chadwick, musingly, 'I don't think the theatre ever fairly took with the Seacomb people. Ours is a serious town, and though there's plenty of spare room in our old parish church—a very fine old church, as you may have seen with your own eyes, but rather in want of repair—there's always a run upon our chapels, revival services, and tea meetings, and love feasts, and what not. People must have excitement of some sort, no doubt, and the Seacomb people like chapel-going better than play-going; besides which it costs them less. I've no prejudices myself, and I know that a theatrical is a human being like myself; but I can't say that I've ever cared to see theatricals inside my doors.'

'But I suppose you used to go to the theatre sometimes, when there was one?'

'Once in a way I have gone to our theatre, when there was a Bespeak night, or a London star performing, more to please my husband, who was fond of anything in the way of an entertainment, than for my own pleasure.'

'Do you remember the names of the actors whom you saw there?'

'No, I can't call to mind one of them. But if you take any interest in theatricals, go and see Mr. Clipcome, our hairdresser. He'll talk to you for the hour together of our theatre, and the people who've acted there. He never cut my hair in his life that he didn't tell me how he once curled and powdered a wig for the celebrated Miss Foote to act Lady Teazle in. It's his 'obby.'

'Indeed! Then I shall certainly look in upon Mr. Clipcome. Where does he live?'

'In a little court, by the side of Bethlehem Chapel, which was the theatre.'

'Thanks, Mrs. Chadwick,' said Maurice, rising. 'I'll step round to Mr. Clipcome at once, and get him to give me the county crop. I've been running to seed lately. Perhaps you'll be kind enough to order me a little bit of dinner in the coffee-room at half-past six.'

'With pleasure, sir. Any choice?'

'None whatever. I shall walk about your town for a few hours, and get an appetite for anything you like to set before me.'

'A very agreeable gentleman,' thought Mrs. Chadwick, as Maurice strolled out of the bar, 'so chatty and friendly. Doesn't give himself half the airs of your commercial gents, yet any one can see he's altogether superior to them.'

Mr. Clissold strolled through the quiet old town, with its long straggling high street, graced here and there by a picturesque gable or an ancient lattice, but, for the most part, somewhat commonplace. At one point there was a kind of square, from which two lateral streets diverged—a square with a pump and police office in the centre, and a Methodist chapel on each side. One of these chapels, the newest and smartest, was Bethlehem, as an inscription over its portal made known to the world at

large—Bethlehem, 1853,—and at the side of Bethlehem, once the Temple of Thespis, there was a clean
paved alley, leading to another street; an alley with
a public-house at one corner, and a few **decent shops**
on one side, facing the blank wall of the chapel.
One of these shops **was** the emporium of Mr. Clipcome, **who was at once** tobacconist, hairdresser,
and **dealer** in fancy and miscellaneous articles too
numerous to mention.

Maurice found Mr. Clipcome standing upon his
threshold contemplating **life as** exhibited **in Play-**
house Court, where **a small** child in a go-cart, and **a**
woman cheapening bloaters at the greengrocer's were
the only objects that presented themselves at this
particular **time to the** student of **humanity.** But
then Mr. Clipcome had an oblique view of the
square, town pump, and police station, **and in a**
general way could see anything that was going on
from the vantage-ground of his door-step.

He was an elderly man, stout, and comfortable
looking, **but** balder than he ought to have been considering **the resources of his art,** and that he was
himself the inventor of an infallible cure for baldness.

But he may have preferred that smooth and shining surface as cooler and more comfortable than capillary embellishment. He wore a clean linen apron, with a comb or two stuck in the pocket thereof—an apron that was in itself an invitation to the passing pedestrian to have his hair cut. On seeing Mr. Clissold making for his door, Mr. Clipcome stepped aside with a smile and a bow, and made way for the stranger to enter his abode.

It was a very small abode, consisting of a shop and a little slip of a parlour behind it, both the pink of neatness, and both agreeably perfumed with hair oil and lavender water. There was a shining arm-chair with a high back, whereon the patient sat enthroned during the hair-cutting process. A looking-glass squeezed into an angle of the parlour reflected patient and operator. A pincushion hung beside it, balanced by a smart chintz bag, containing a variety of implements. But the object which most struck Maurice's eye was an old playbill, smaller than modern playbills, and yellow with age, framed and glazed, and hanging against the wall, just as if it had been some choice work of art.

It was the programme of a performance of 'Othello' that had taken place early in the century. 'Othello, the Moor of Venice, Mr. Kean.'

'You remember the great Kean?' said Maurice.'

'Yes, sir,' answered Mr. Clipcome, with pride. 'I remember Edmund Kean, and I remember Charles Young, and Miss O'Neil, and Miss Foote, and Mrs. Nesbitt, and Mr. Macready, and a good deal more talent such as you're not likely to see in these days. Seacomb Theatre was worth going to in my boyhood.'

'And you were an enthusiastic patron of the drama, I imagine?'

'If spending every sixpence of my pocket-money upon admission to the pit is a proof of enthusiasm, I was an enthusiast, sir,' replied Mr. Clipcome. 'The sixpences which boys—well, I will venture to say boys of an inferior mind—would have laid out upon cakes and apples, peg-tops, and such like, I spent upon the drama. There's hardly a line of Shakespeare you could quote that I couldn't cap with another line. I used to go to the pit of that theatre twice a week while I was a youngster, and three or four times a week after my father's death, when I was in business for myself and my own master, and used to get a weekly order for exhibiting the bills. And though there were a good many opposed to the closing of the theatre for ever, I don't believe there was any one in all Seacomb took it to heart as keenly as I did. "Othello's occupation was gone." '

'Why did they do away with your theatre at last?' asked Maurice.

' Well, you see, sir, the town had grown serious-minded, and for some years before they turned it into a chapel the theatre had been going down. The great actors and actresses were dead and gone, and the stars that were left didn't care about coming to Seacomb. Managers had been doing worse and worse year after year, business dwindling down to next to nothing, half salaries, or no salaries towards the end of every season, and it became a recognised fact in the theatrical profession that Seacomb was no go. The actors and actresses that came here were sticks, or if not, they made up in rant what they wanted in talent. The county families left off coming to the place—there were no Bespeaks, and the poor old theatre got to have a dilapidated woebegone look, so that it gave one the horrors to sit out a play. The actors looked hungry and out at elbows. It made one uncomfortable to see them. Many a time I asked one of them in to share my one o'clock dinner, if it was but a potato pasty, or a squab pie made with scrag of mutton. The stage door used to be just opposite my shop. It's walled up now, but you may see the outline of it in the brickwork. The actors used to be always lounging about that doorway of a morning, on and off, and whilst the rehearsal was going on inside. And they were very fond of coming into my shop for a gossip, or a peep at a newspaper. Papers were dear in those days. No *Standard* or *Telegraph* with all the news of the world for a penny. And the poor chaps couldn't afford to lay out fivepence.'

'You must have been on friendly terms with a good many of them,' said Maurice, feeling that from this loquacious barber, if from any one in Seacomb, he was likely to obtain the information he sought. 'Do you happen to remember a man called Elgood?'

' Elgood ! Mat Elgood,' cried the operator, dropping his scissors in the vehemence of his exclamation, ' I should think I did indeed ! He was one who hung on to our Theatre Royal to the very last, —stuck to it like a barnacle, poor fellow,—when there was not enough sustenance to be got out of it to keep body and soul together. He lodged in this very court, the last house on the other side, next door but one to the Theatre—a tailor's it was then— and a good little man the tailor was, and a kind friend to Mat Elgood—as long as he had a crust to share with him, or a garret to shelter him. But one day, about a month after the theatre had shut up shop altogether, the manager having bolted—the brokers walked into poor Jones's little place and took possession of everything, and Jones went to prison, so Mat Elgood and his wife, a poor weak thing that had lost her first baby only a few weeks before that time, were cast loose upon the world, and what became of them from that hour to this I never heard. If I'd had an empty room in my house I'd have given it them, but I hadn't, and my wife is a prudent woman, who never forgot to remind me that my first duty was to her and my children, or, in other words, that charity begins at home.'

'Do you remember the date of this occurrence—the year and month in which Matthew Elgood left Seacomb? I may as well tell you that I do not ask these questions out of idle curiosity. I am personally interested in knowing all about this Mr. Elgood.'

'My dear sir,' exclaimed the barber, swelling with importance at the idea of giving valuable information, 'you could not have come to a better source. If I fail to remember the dates you require, I can produce documentary evidence which will place the fact beyond all doubt. For a period of ten years or upwards I made it a rule to keep a copy of every playbill issued in our town. They were delivered at my door gratis for exhibition in my window, and instead of throwing them aside as waste paper, I filed them as interesting records for re-perusal in the leisure of my later life. I am rather proud of that collection. It contains the name of many a brilliant light in the dramatic hemisphere, and, indeed, I look upon it as a history of dramatic art in little. My impression is that Elgood and his wife left Seacomb nineteen years ago last winter, but the bills will make matters certain. Matthew Elgood was among that diminished band which trod the boards of our poor little theatre on that final night when the green curtain descended on the Seacomb stage, never to rise again. The theatre remained in abeyance for some two or three years after that last performance, dismantled, shut up, a refuge for rats and mice, and such small deer.'

'Nineteen years ago, you say?'

'Nor more nor less,' returned Mr. Clipcome, who was wont to wax Shakesperian. 'I remember it was an extraordinary severe winter. We had frost and snow, a great deal of snow, as late as the end of February, and even into March. Some of the roads between Seacomb and neighbouring villages were impassable, and there was a good deal of trouble generally. I felt all the more for those unfortunate Elgoods on this account,—it was a hard winter in which to be cast adrift.'

'Thanks, Mr. Clipcome, you have given me really valuable information. I should be glad to refer to that file of bills, so as to get the exact date of the closing of the theatre.'

The hairdresser produced his collection, roughly bound in a ponderous marble-paper covered tome, of his own manufacture, a triumph in amateur book-binding. Here Maurice saw the last play bill that had ever been issued by the manager of the Seacomb theatre. Its date was January 10th, 1849.

'And Mr. Elgood stayed at the tailor's for a month after the closing of the theatre?' interrogated Maurice.

'About a month.'

Having jotted down dates and facts in his note-book, and reiterated his thanks to the good-natured barber, Maurice felt that his business in Playhouse Alley was concluded. He bought some trifles in the shop, on his way out, an attention peculiarly pleasing to Mr. Clipcome, from the rarity of the event, his trade being chiefly confined to two-penny-worths of hair oil, or three-halfpenny cakes of brown Windsor.

CHAPTER VII.

A QUIET evening at the 'New London Inn,' and another confidential chat with its proprietress convinced Maurice that there was nothing more to be learned in Seacomb. He led Mrs. Chadwick on to talk of the family at Penwyn Manor House, the old Squire and his sons, who, sanctified by the shadows of the past, beautified by old memories and associations—just as a ruin is beautified by the ivies and lichens that cling to its crumbling arches —were dearer to the hearts of the elderly Seacombites than the reigning Squire and his lovely wife.

'I don't say but what the present gentleman is better for trade, and has done more good to the neighbourhood in two years than the old Squire would have done in ten,' said Mrs. Chadwick.

'But the old Squire was more one of ourselves, as you may say. He'd take his glass of cider—a very temperate man was the Squire—in my bar parlour, and chat with me as friendly and familiar as you could do, and it was quite a pleasant thing to see him, in his Lincoln green coat and brass basket buttons, and mahogany tops.'

Of George Penwyn Mrs. Chadwick said nothing that was not praise. He had been everybody's favourite, she told Maurice, and his death had been felt like a personal loss throughout the neighbourhood.

Was this a man to betray an innocent girl, and bring disgrace upon an honest yeoman's household?

Before leaving Seacomb next morning Mr. Clissold went to the parish church, looked once more at the register in which he had seen the baptism of Matthew Elgood's daughter; and afterwards referred to the register of burials to assure himself of the child's death. There was the entry : 'Emily Jane, daughter of Matthew Elgood, comedian, and Jane Elgood, his wife, aged five weeks.

January 4th, 1849.'　　Just six days before the closing of the Seacomb Theatre.

Maurice distinctly remembered Justina having told him once, in the course of their somewhat discursive talk, that her birthday was in March, and that she had completed her nineteenth year on her last anniversary. Now, if Mrs. Elgood had had a daughter born in the December of 1848, it was not possible for her to have been the mother of Justina, if Justina was born in the March of 1849.

He had now no shadow of doubt that Matthew Elgood, who had left Seacomb in February in the midst of frost and snow, was the same man who had sought shelter at Borcel End, and who had called himself Eden. A false pride had doubtless induced the penniless stroller to hide his poverty under an assumed name.

'The plainest, most straightforward way of doing things will be to tax Elgood himself with the fact,' thought Maurice. 'Once sure of my darling's identity with Muriel's daughter, my next duty shall be to discover the evidence of her mother's marriage. And if I succeed in doing that——?

Well, I suppose the next thing will be for some clever lawyers to prove her right to the Penwyn estate, and Churchill Penwyn and his wife will be ruined, and Justina will be a great heiress, and I shall retire into the background. Hardly a pleasant picture of the future, that. Perhaps it would have been wiser, from a purely selfish point of view, to have left my dear girl Justina Elgood to the end of the chapter—or at least till I persuaded her to exchange that spurious surname for the good old name of Clissold. But now having gone so far, won the confidence of a dying woman, sworn to set right an old wrong, I am in honour bound to go on, not to the ultimate issue, perhaps, but at any rate to the assertion of my darling girl's legitimacy.

He rejoiced in the swiftness of the express which carried him homewards, by stubble fields, and yellowing woods, rejoiced at the thought that he should be in time to see Justina, were it only one half-hour before she went to the theatre. He took a hansom and drove straight to Hudspeth Street, told the man to wait, and left his portmanteau and travelling bag in the cab while he ran upstairs to the second floor sitting-room.

Matthew Elgood was enjoying his afternoon siesta, his amiable countenance shrouded from the autumnal fly by a crimson silk handkerchief. Justina was sitting at a little table by the window, reading.

She looked a shade paler than when he had seen her last, the lover thought, fondly hoping that she had missed him, but as she started up from her chair, recognising him with a little cry of gladness, the warm blood rushed to cheek and brow, and he had no ground for compassionating her pallor.

For a moment she tried to speak, but could not, and in that moment Maurice knew that he was beloved.

He would have given worlds to take her to his heart, then and there, to have kissed the blushes into a deeper glow, to have told her how supremely dear she was to him, how infinitely deeper, and holier, and sweeter than his first foolish passion this second love of his had become. But he put the curb on impulse, remembering the task he had to accomplish. To woo her now, to win her promise now, knowing what he knew, would have seemed to him a meanness.

'To-day I am her superior in fortune,' he said to himself, 'a year hence I may be her inferior— a very pauper compared with the mistress of Penwyn Manor. I will not win her unawares. If change of fortune does come to pass I shall not be too proud to share her wealth, so long as I have all her heart ; but if she should change with change of fortune, she shall be free to follow where her fancy leads, and no old promise, made in her day of obscurity, shall bind her to me. Free and unfettered she shall enter upon her new life.

So instead of taking her to his heart of hearts, and pouring out his tale of love in a tender whisper—too low to penetrate the crimson handkerchief which veiled the ears of the sleeper, Maurice greeted Justina with hearty loudness, talked about his journey—asked how the new piece at the Albert worked out at rehearsal—inquired about his friend Flittergilt, the dramatist—and behaved altogether in a commonplace fashion. There was just time for a cup of tea before Justina started for the theatre—and a very pleasant tea-drinking it was. Maurice was touched by Justina's pretty joyous ways this evening, her bright looks, the silvery little laugh gushing out at the slightest provocation, —laughter which told of a soul that was gladdened by his presence.

'I think I shall come to the theatre to-night,' he said, as they parted.

'What, to see "No Cards"? You must be dreadfully tired of it.'

'No. I believe I have seen it seven times, but I could see it seven more,' answered Maurice, and this was the only compliment he paid Justina that evening. Before parting with Mr. Elgood, he asked that gentleman to dine with him the next evening, at eight, *en garçon.*

'We can go to the theatre afterwards to escort Miss Elgood home,' he added.

'My dear Clissold,' exclaimed the comedian, with effusion, 'after the bottle of port you gave me that Sunday evening, Justina and I enjoyed your hospitality, I should be an ass to refuse such an invitation.'

CHAPTER VIII.

NOTHING could be more inviting than the aspect of Maurice Clissold's rooms at eight o'clock on the following evening, when their proprietor stood on his hearth, waiting the arrival of his expected guest. The weather was by no means warm, and the glass and silver on the friendly-looking circular table sparkled in the glow of a brightly burning fire. The spotless damask, the dainty arrangement of the table, with its old Chelsea ware dessert dishes, filled with amber-tinted Jersey pears, and dusky-hued filberts, agreeably suggestive of good old port, indicated a careful landlady and well-trained servants. The dumb-waiter, with its reserve of glasses and cruets, guaranteed that luxurious ease which is not dependent on external service.

Mr. Elgood, arriving on the scene as the clocks of

Bloomsbury struck the hour, surveyed these preparations with an eye that glistened with content—nay, almost brightened to rapture—as it wandered from the table to the fender, where, in a shadowy corner, reposed the expected bottle of port, cobweb-wreathed, chalk-marked.

The savoury odour of fried fish, mingled with the appetising fumes of roasting meat, had greeted the visitor's nostrils as he ascended the stairs. Even his nice judgment had failed to divine whether the joint were beef or mutton, but he opined mutton. No one but a barbarian would load his table with sirloin for a *tête-à-tête* dinner when Providence had created the Welsh hills, doubtless with a view to the necessities of the dinner-table.

' Glad to see you so punctual,' said Maurice, cheerily.

' My dear Mr. Clissold, to be unpunctual is to insult one's host and injure one's self. What can atone for the ruin of an excellent dinner ? You may remember what Dean Swift said to his cook when she had roasted the joint to rags, and was fain to confess she could not undo the evil : " Beware wench, how you commit a fault which cannot be remedied." A dinner spoiled is an irremediable loss.'

The soup had been put upon the table while Mr. Elgood thus philosophized, so the two gentlemen sat down without further delay, and the comedian gazed blandly upon the amber sherry and the garnet-hued claret, while Maurice invoked a blessing on the feast, and then the business of dinner began in good earnest.

The joint was mutton, and Welsh, whereby Mr. Elgood's soul was at ease, and he gave himself up to the enjoyment of the table with unaffected singleness of purpose. A brace of partridges and a Parmesan *fondu* followed the haunch ; and when these had been despatched the comedian flung himself back in his chair, with a sigh of repletion.

' Well, my dear Mr. Clissold,' he said, ' you are a very accomplished gentleman in many ways ; but this I will say, that I never met the man yet who was your match in giving a snug little dinner. Brilsby Savory, or whatever his name was, couldn't have beat you.'

' I am glad you have enjoyed your dinner, Mr.

Elgood. I am of opinion that a good dinner is the best prelude to a serious conversation ; and I want to have a little quiet and confidential talk with you this evening upon a very serious matter.'

' Behold me at your service,—your slave to command,' answered Matthew, whose enthusiasm was not easily to be damped. 'I bare my bosom to your view,' he added, with a dramatic gesture, indicative of throwing open his waistcoat.

They were alone by this time. The servant had carried away the dinner-things, and only the decanters and fruit dishes remained on the table.

'You speak boldly, Mr. Elgood,' said Maurice, with sudden gravity, 'yet, perhaps, if I were to ask you some questions about your past life you would draw back a little.'

' My past life, although full of vicissitude, has been honest,' answered the comedian. 'I fear no man's scrutiny.'

' Good. Then you will not be angry if I question you rather closely upon one period of your chequered career. It is in the interest of your—of Justina that I do so.'

'Proceed, sir,' said Matthew, a troubled look overclouding the countenance which had just now beamed with serenity.

'Did you ever hear the name of Eden?'

Mr. Elgood started, more violently than he had done on a previous occasion at the mention of Borcel End. The silver dessert knife with which he was pealing a Jersey pear dropped from between his fingers.

'I see you do know that name,' said Maurice, passing from interrogation to affirmation. 'You bore it once at Borcel End, the old farm house on the Cornish moors, where you took shelter in bitter winter weather, just nineteen years ago last February.'

The glow which the good things of this life had kindled in Mr. Elgood's visage faded slowly out, and left him very pale.

'How did you know that?' he gasped.

'I had it from the lips of a dying woman—Mrs. Trevanard.'

'What! is Mrs. Trevanard dead?'

'Yes; she died a fortnight ago.'

'And she told you—— ?'

'All. The birth of the child she entrusted to your care. The old family Bible she gave you, from which you took the name of Justina.'

The shrewd guess, stated as a fact, passed uncontradicted. Maurice's speculative assertion had hit the truth.

'The supposed daughter who has borne your name all these years, the girl who has worked for you, who now maintains you, who has been faithful, obedient, and devoted to you, has not one drop of your blood in her veins. She is Muriel Trevanard's child.'

'You choose to make a statement,' said Matthew Elgood, who had somewhat recovered his self-possession by this time, 'which I do not feel myself called upon either to deny or admit. I am willing to acknowledge that in a time of severe misfortune I took shelter upon Mrs. Trevanard's premises; that I called myself by a name that was not my own, rather than expose my destitution to the world's contumely. But whatever passed between Mrs. Trevanard and myself at that period is sacred. I swore to keep the secret confided to me to my dying

day, and it will descend with me to the tomb of my
ancestors,' added Mr. Elgood, grandly, as if, for the
moment at least, he really believed that he had a
family vault at his disposal.

'You may consider yourself absolved of your
oath,' said Maurice. 'Mrs. Trevanard confided in
me during the last days of her life, and I pledged
myself to see her grandchild righted.'

'Mrs. Trevanard must have changed very much
at the last if she expressed any interest in the fate
of her grandchild,' returned Matthew, forgetting that
he had refused to make any admission. 'When she
gave the child to me and my wife, she resigned all
concern in its future: it was to fare as we fared, to
sink or swim with us.'

'In that wretched hour she thought the child
nameless and fatherless. I did my best to persuade
her that she had been too hasty in her conclusion.
It shall be my business to prove Justina's legitimacy.'

'That is to say, you mean to take my daughter
away from me,' exclaimed the comedian, wrathfully.
'Little did I know what a snake in the grass I had

been cherishing, warming the adder in my bosom,
sheltering the scorpion on my domestic hearth.
This is what your kettle-drums, and snug little
dinners, and port and filberts, are to end in. You
would rob a poor old man of the staff and comfort
of his declining years : six pounds a week, and a
certainty of a rise to ten if the next part she plays
is a success.'

'You are hasty, Mr. Elgood, and unjust. Believe me, if it were a question of my own happiness,
I would leave the dear girl you have brought up,
Justina Elgood, till I had the Archbishop of Canter-
bury's permission to give her my own name. But,
having promised to perform a certain duty, I should
be a scoundrel if I left it undone. What if I tell
you that I have reason to believe Justina entitled
to a large estate, an estate of six or seven thousand
a year ?'

Mr. Elgood sank back in his chair aghast. He
had drunk a good many glasses of wine in the
course of that comfortable little dinner, and there
was some slight haziness in his brain. Six thousand
a year, six pounds a week. Six pounds a week, six

thousand a year—over a hundred pounds a week. There was a wide margin for spending in the difference between the lesser and greater sum. But of the six pounds a week, while Justina supposed herself his daughter, he was certain. Would she share her annual six thousand as freely when she knew that he had no claim upon her filial piety ?'

He pondered the question for a few moments, and then answered it in the affirmative. Generous, good, loving, she had ever been. If good fortune befell her she would not grudge the old man his share of the sunshine. He had not been a bad father to her, he told himself, take him for all in all—not over-patient, or considerate, perhaps, in those early days, before he had discovered any dramatic talent in her ; a little prone to think of his own comfort before hers ; but upon the whole, as fathers go, not a bad kind of parent. And he felt very sure she would stand by him. Yes, he felt sure of Justina. But he must be on his guard against this scheming fellow, Clissold, who had contrived to get hold of a secret that had been kept for nineteen years, and doubtless meant to work it for his own advantage. It would be Matthew Elgood's duty to countermarch him here.

'So, Mr. Clissold,' he began, after about five minutes' reverie, 'you are a pretty deep fellow, you are, in spite of your easy, open-handed, open-hearted, free-spoken ways. You think you can establish my Justina's claim to a fine fortune, do you? And I suppose, when the claim is established, and the girl I have brought up from babyhood, and toiled for and struggled for many a long year, comes into her six thousand per annum, you'll expect to get her for your wife, with the six or seven thousand at her back. Rather a good stroke of business for you!'

'I expect nothing,' answered Maurice, gravely. 'I love Justina with all my heart, as truly as ever an honest man loved a fair and noble woman; but I have refrained from any expression of my heart's desire, lest I should bind her by a promise while her position is thus uncertain. Let her win the station to which I believe she is entitled; and if, when it is won, she cares to reward my honest affection, I will take her and be proud of her; but not one whit prouder than I should be to take her for my wife to-morrow, knowing her to be your daughter.'

'Spoken like a man and a gentleman,' exclaimed the comedian. 'Come, Mr. Clissold, I couldn't think badly of you if I tried. I'll trust you; and it shall be no fault of mine if Justina is not yours, rich or poor. She's worthy of you, and you're worthy of her, and I believe she has a sneaking kindness for you.'

Maurice smiled, happy in a conviction which needed no support from Matthew Elgood's opinion. That little look of Justina's yesterday—that tender look of greeting—had been worth volumes of pro-testation. He knew himself beloved.

'And now tell me what your ideas are; and how Mrs. Trevanard—the strangest woman, and the closest that I ever met—came to confide in you, and how it has entered into your mind that our Justina has any legal right to either name or fortune.'

'I'll tell you, said Maurice, and forthwith pro-ceeded to relate all that he had learned at Borcel, a great deal of which was new to Matthew Elgood, who had been told nothing about the parentage of the child committed to his care. It was essential to Justina's interests that her adopted father should know all, since he was the only witness who could prove her identity with the child born at Borcel End.

'It seems tolerably clear that this George Penwyn must have been the father,' said Mr. Elgood. 'But who is to prove a marriage?'

'If a marriage took place, the proof must exist somewhere, and it must be for one of us to find it,' answered Maurice. 'The first person to apply to is Miss Barlow, Muriel's schoolmistress, supposing her to be still living. The only period of Muriel's absence from the farm after she left school was the time she spent with Miss Barlow—three weeks—so that if any marriage took place it must have happened during that visit. I have searched the registers of both churches at Seacomb without result. But it is not likely that George Penwyn would contract a secret marriage within a few miles of his father's house. Whatever occurred in those three weeks Miss Barlow must have been in some measure familiar with. My first business therefore must be to find her.   When last heard of she was established as a teacher of music in the neighbourhood of London.   A directory ought to help us to her address, if she is still living within the postal radius.'

'True,' said Matthew, glancing at the shelves which lined the room from floor to ceiling. 'I suppose among all these books you have the Post Office Directory?'

'No, strange to say, it is a branch of literature I am deficient in.   I must wait till to-morrow to look for Miss Barlow's address.'

'How did it occur to you that my daughter Justina and that castaway child were one and the same?'

'Well, I hardly know how the idea first took possession of me. It was a kind of instinct. The circumstances that led me to think it seemed insignificant enough when spoken of, but to my mind they assumed exaggerated importance; perhaps it was your look of surprise when I mentioned Borcel End that first awakened my suspicions, not of the actual truth, but of some mysterious connection between yourself and the Trevanards.'

'I certainly was astonished when you spoke of that out-of-the-way farm house.'

'Then the name Justina, which I heard of as a family name at Borcel End, that set me thinking; the fact that your daughter was said to have been born at Seacomb, within a few miles of that remote farmhouse; the fact that her age tallied with the age of Muriel's child. Never mind how I came by the conviction, since I happily, or unhappily, stumbled on the truth. But tell me how you fared when you left Borcel End that bleak spring morning?'

'Well, it wasn't the most comfortable kind of departure, certainly—four miles on foot on a cold March morning, and an infant to carry into the bargain. But my poor wife and I had gone through too much to be particular about trifles, and we were both of us sustained by the thought of a snug little fortune in my breast pocket; for you may suppose that to us two hundred pounds odd seemed the capital of a future Rothschild. Mrs. Trevanard had given us some substantial clothing into the bargain, and my poor Nell wore a good cloth cloak, under which the baby was kept warm and snug. She was stronger, too, my poor girl, for the month's rest and plentiful food that we had enjoyed at Borcel—indeed, though our lodging there was but a deserted hayloft, I don't think either of us was ever happier than when Nell sat at her needlework and I lay luxuriously reposing on a truss of hay, while I read an old magazine aloud to her. We were shut out from the world, but we had peace and rest and plenty; and I think we were pretty much like the birds of the air as to thought of the morrow in those days. But now that I had Mrs. Trevanard's savings in my breast pocket I began to take a serious view of life, and throughout that walk to Seacomb I was scheming and contriving, till at last, just as we came in sight of the town, I cried out in a burst of enthusiasm, " Yes, Nell, I've hit it." " Hit what ? " asked my wife. " Hit upon the surest way to make our fortunes, my girl," I answered, all of a glow with the thought. " We'll take a theatre." " Lor', Mat," said my wife with a gasp, " and I can play the leading business ! " Managers had been putting other women over her head in the Juliets and Rosalinds, and she felt it, poor soul " But Matthew," she went on, growing suddenly serious, " we haven't seen much good come of taking theatres. Look at Seacomb, for instance." " Seacomb isn't a case in point," I answered, quite put out by her narrow way of looking at things. " A psalm-singing place like that was never likely to support the drama. When I take a theatre. it will be in a very different town from Seacomb." " But," remonstrated poor Nell, " don't you think it would be breaking faith with Mrs. Trevanard ? She gave us the money to set us up in some nice little business. We were to start with part of the capital and keep the rest in reserve against a rainy day." " Well, isn't theatrical management a business ?" I retorted, " and the only business that I am fit for. Do you suppose that I can blossom into a full-blown grocer, or break out all at once into a skilful butcher, because Mrs. Trevanard wishes it ? Why, I shouldn't know one end of an ox from the other when his head was off. And as for Mrs. Trevanard," I went on, " you ought to have sense enough to know that she cares precious little what becomes of us now we've taken this unfortunate child off her hands." " I don't believe that, Matthew," answered my wife, " she's a

Christian, and she wouldn't like us to starve on the child's account." "Who's going to starve?" I cried, savagely, for I felt it was in me to make money as a manager. There never was an actor yet that hadn't the same fancy, and many a man has brought ruin upon himself and his family by the delusion.'

'You had your own way, of course?' said Maurice.

'I had, sir. First and foremost my poor little wife never obstinately opposed me in anything; and secondly, her foolish heart was longing for the leading business, and to be a manageress, and cast all the pieces, and put herself in for the best parts. So we went straight to the Seacomb station, where we found we should have to wait upwards of an hour for a train, and I thought I could not make better use of my time than by buying an *Era*, and finding out what theatres were to let. There were about half a dozen advertisements of this class, and one of them struck me as the exact thing. " The Theatre Royal, Slowberry, Somersetshire, to let for the summer season. Rent moderate. Can be worked with a small company. Scenery in good condition.

Market town ; population twelve thousand." I made a calculation on the spot, demonstrating that ten per cent. of those twelve thousand inhabitants—allowing a wide margin for infants, the aged, and infirm—were bound to come to the theatre nightly. Now a nightly audience of twelve hundred was safe to pay. I found that we could get straight to Slowberry by the Great Western, and accordingly took tickets for that station, third class, for prudence was to be the order of the day. Well, Mr. Clissold, I need not trouble you with details. We went to Slowberry, and established ourselves in humble and inexpensive lodgings, apartments which I felt were hardly worthy of my managerial position, but prudence prevailed. I became lessee of the Slowberry theatre, which I am fain to admit was in architectural pretensions even below the Temple of the Drama at Seacomb. I engaged my company, cheap and useful. My old man combined the heavy business and second low comedy; my first chambermaid—second I need hardly say there was none—danced or sang between the pieces, and acted in male attire when we ran short of gentlemen. My wife and I played all the best parts.   Nothing could have been organized upon more rigid principles of economy, yet the financial result was ruin.   For a considerable part of the season I only paid half salaries, for the concluding portion we became a commonwealth. Yet Mrs. Trevanard's savings dribbled away, and, when my poor wife and I left Slowberry, with Justina—then a fine child of seven months old, —we had not twenty pounds left out of a capital which had appeared to my mind to be almost inexhaustible.

'The child was christened at Slowberry, I suppose?'

'Yes, we lost no time in having the baptismal rite performed, lest she should go off with croup, or red-gum, or vaccination, or any of the perils which beset the infant traveller on life's thorny road. The Bible which Mrs. Trevanard had given to my wife contained in the fly-leaf the name of Justina Trevanard, doubtless its original possessor.   That name caught my wife's fancy.   It struck me, also, as euphonious and aristocratic, a name that would look well in the bills by and by, when our daughter

was old enough to make her first juvenile efforts
in the profession, as the child in " Pizarro," or little
William in "The Stranger." We were fond of her
already, and soon grew to forget that there was no
tie of kindred between us. My wife indeed passionately adored this nameless orphan, and was never tired
of weaving romantic fancies about her future, how
she would turn out to be the daughter of a nobleman,
and we should see her by and by with a coronet on
her head, and owe comfort and wealth to her affection when we grew old. It would be a curious thing
if one of poor Nell's romantic dreams were to be
realized. How proud that loving heart would have
been ! but it lies under the grass and daisies in a
Berkshire churchyard, and neither joy nor sorrow
can touch it any more.'

Mr. Elgood checked a rising sigh, and helped
himself to another glass of port.

' You fared ill, I fear, after your managerial experi-
ment,' said Maurice.

' Our life from that point was a series of struggles.
If the efforts of the honest man battling with adver-
sity form a spectacle which the gods delight in—a

fact which I vaguely remember having seen stated somewhere—my career must have afforded considerable entertainment in Olympus. We had our brief intervals of sunshine, but cloud prevailed ; and in the course of years my poor wife sank beneath the burden, and Justina and I were left to jog on together, just as you saw us in the town of Eborsham two years ago. So far as a struggler can do his duty to his daughter, I believe I did mine to Justina. I gave her what little education I could afford, and luckily she was bright enough to make the most of that little. There never was such a girl for picking up knowledge. Clever people always seemed to take to her, and she to them, though for a long time we thought her stupid on the stage. Her talent for the profession came out all at once. Heaven knows, she has been a good girl to me, through good and evil fortune, and I love her as well as if she were twenty times my daughter. It would be a hard thing if any change of circumstances were to part us.'

'Have no fear of that,' said Maurice. 'Justina is too true a woman to be changed by changing fortune. I do not hesitate to leave my fate in her hands. You, who have an older claim upon her love, have even less cause for fear.'

The little black marble clock on the mantelpiece chimed the half-hour after ten—time to repair to the theatre. Mr. Flittergilt's piece ended at a quarter before eleven, and at a few minutes past the hour Justina appeared at the stage door, ready to be escorted home.

Maurice and Mr. Elgood went together to the dark little side street in which the stage door of the Royal Albert was situated, dingy and repellent of aspect after the manner of stage doors.

It was a starlight autumn night, and that walk back to Bloomsbury with Justina's little hand resting on his own arm was very pleasant to Maurice Clissold. They chose the quietest streets, without reference to distance, and the walk lasted about a quarter of an hour longer than it need have done had they gratified Mr. Elgood's predilection for certain short cuts, by Wych Street and Drury Lane. But throughout that homeward walk not one whispered word of Maurice's betrayed the lover, and when he and Justina parted at the door of her lodgings, the girl thought wonderingly of that summer night in Eborsham, more than two years ago, when James Penwyn told her of his love in the shadow of the old minster.

'Shall I ever have a second lover as generous and devoted?' she mused. 'That was only boy and girl love, I suppose, yet it seemed truer and brighter than anything that will ever come my way again.'

She had been thinking of Maurice not a little of late, and had decided that he did not care for her in the least.

CHAPTER IX.

'THE DAYS HAVE VANISHED, TONE AND TINT.'

MAURICE CLISSOLD lost no time in setting about his search for Miss Barlow, the quondam schoolmistress of Seacomb. But the first result of his endeavours was a failure. The London Post Office Directory for the current year knew not Miss Barlow. Barlows there were in its pages, but they were trading Barlows; Barlows who baked, or Barlows who brewed; Barlows who dealt in upholstery; Barlows who purveyed butcher's meat; or professional Barlows, who wrote Rev. before or M.R.C.S. after their names. A spinster of the musical profession was not to be found among the London Barlows.

In the face of this disappointment Maurice paused to consider his next effort. Advertising in the *Times* he looked upon as a last resource, and a means of inquiry which he hoped to dispense with.

So many spurious Miss Barlows eager to hear of something to their advantage, would be conjured into being by any appeal published in the second column of the *Times*.

There remained to him the detective medium, but Maurice cherished a prejudice against private inquiry offices, and would not for all the wealth of this realm have revealed Muriel's story to a professional detective. He was resolved to succeed or fail in this business single-handed.

'If Miss Barlow is above ground her existence must be known to somebody,' he reasoned, 'to musical people more particularly. I'll go down to the Albert Theatre and have a chat with the leader of the orchestra. Your musical director is generally a man of the world, with a little more than the average amount of brains. And I have heard Justina speak very highly of Herr Fisfiz. Flittergilt's new comedy is in rehearsal, so I have an excuse for going behind the scenes.'

It was about noon on the day after his little entertainment to Mr. Elgood that Maurice arrived at this decision. He went straight from his club, where he had explored the Court Guide and Postal Directory, to the snug little theatre in the Strand, where, after some parley with the stage doorkeeper, he obtained admittance, and groped his way through subterranean regions of outer darkness, and by some breakneck stairs, to the side scenes, where, in a dim glimmer of daylight and fitful glare of gas, he beheld the stage on one side of him, and the open door of the green-room on the other.

Justina was rehearsing. Mr. Flittergilt, in a state of mental fever, sat by the stage manager's little table, manuscript and pencil in hand, under-lining here, erasing there, now altering an exit, now suggesting the proper emphasis to give point to a sparkling sentence, evidently delighted with his own work, yet as evidently painfully anxious about the result.

'I shan't be satisfied with a moderate success,' he told Maurice. 'I want this piece to make a greater hit than "No Cards." You remember what was said of Sheridan when he hung back from writing a new comedy. He was afraid of the author of "The Rivals." Now I don't want that to be said of *me.*'

'No fear, dear boy,' remarked Maurice. But Mr. Flittergilt's exalted mind ignored the interjection.

'I want the public to see that I have not emptied my sack; that "No Cards" was not my ace of trumps, but only my knave. I've queen, king, and ace to follow! Did you hear the last scene?" asked the author, with a self-satisfied smile. 'It's rather sparkling, I think; and Elgood hits the character to the life.'

Mr. Clissold did not approve this familiar allusion to the girl of his choice.

'I've only just this moment come in,' he said; 'I'm glad Miss Elgood likes her new *rôle.*'

'Likes it?' cried Flittergilt, with an injured look. 'It wouldn't be easy for any actress on the boards not to like such a part. "No Cards" made Miss Elgood; but this piece will place her a step higher on the ladder.'

'Don't you think there may be people weak-minded enough to believe that Miss Elgood's acting made "No Cards"?' asked Maurice, quietly.

'I can't help people's weak-mindedness,' answered

Mr. Flittergilt, with dignity; 'but I know this for a fact, that no acting—not of a Macready or a Faucit —ever made a bad piece run over a hundred nights.' And with this assertion of himself Mr. Flittergilt went back to his table and his manuscript, and began to badger the actors—being possessed by the idea that because he was able to construct a play from the various foreign materials at his command, he must necessarily be able to teach experienced comedians their art.

Justina looked up from her book presently, and espied Mr. Clissold. Her blush betrayed surprise, her eyes revealed that the surprise was not un-pleasant.

'Have you come to criticise the new comedy?' she asked. 'That's hardly fair, though, for a piece loses so much at rehearsal. Mr. Flittergilt is always calling us back to give us his own peculiar reading of a line. I never saw such an excitable little man. But I suppose he'll take things more coolly when he has written a few more plays.'

'Yes; he is new to the work as yet. I am glad to hear you have such a good part.'

'It is a wonderfully good part, if I can only act it as it ought to be played.'

'Is your leader, Herr Fisfiz, here this morning?' asked Maurice.

'He is coming presently. There's a gavotte in the third act.'

'You dance?'

'Yes, Mr. Mortimer and I. Herr Fisfiz has written original music for it—so quaint and pretty. You should stay to hear it, now you are here.'

'I mean to stay till the rehearsal is over. I should like you to introduce me to Mr. Fisfiz; I want to ask him a question or two about some musical people.

'I shall be pleased to introduce you to each other. He is a very clever man, not in music only, but in all kinds of things, and I think you would like him.'

Maurice seated himself in a dark corner, near the prompter's box, and awaited Mr. Fisfiz, amusing himself by listening to the comedy, and beholding his friend Flittergilt's frantic exertions in the meanwhile. He had been thus occupied nearly an hour when Mr. Fisfiz appeared, attended by his *ame damnée* in the person of the *répétiteur*. The director was a little man, with a small delicate face, and a Shakesperian brow; spoke English perfectly, though with a German accent, and had no dislike to hearing himself talk, or to wasting a stray half-hour in the society of a pretty actress, or even bestowing the sunshine of his presence for a few leisure minutes on a group of giggling ballet-girls. He was evidently a great admirer of Miss Elgood, and inclined to be gracious to any one she introduced to him.

'I think you'll like the gafotte,' he said, playing little pizzicato passages on his violin, with a satisfied smile. 'It sounds like Bach.'

Justina told him it was charming. The dance began presently, and though she only walked through it, the grace of her movements charmed that silent lover of hers, who sat in his corner and made no sign, lest in uttering the most common-place compliment he should betray that secret which he had pledged himself to keep.

When the gavotte was finished, Justina brought Herr Fisfiz to the dark corner, and left him there with Maurice, while she went on with her rehearsal.

Mr. Clissold gave the gavotte its meed of praise, said a few words about things in general, and then came to the question he wanted to ask.

'There is a lady connected with the musical profession I am trying to find,' he said, 'and it struck me this morning that you might be able to assist me.'

'I know most people in the musical world,' answered Herr Fisfiz. 'What is the lady's name?'

'Miss Barlow.'

'Miss Barlow. How do you spell the name?'

Maurice spelt it, and the director shook his head.

'I know no one of that name. No Miss B-a-r-l-o-w,' he said. 'I never heard of any one so called in the musical profession. Is your Miss Barlow a concert singer? Young—an amateur, perhaps, who has not yet made herself known?'

She is not a concert singer, and she must be middle-aged—probably elderly. The last account I have of her goes back to ten years ago. She may be dead and gone for anything I know to the contrary ; but I have heard that she was living in or near London ten years ago, giving lessons in music, and that she was doing well. She was a retired schoolmistress, and had made money, therefore was not likely to go in for ill-paid drudgery She must have had some standing in her profession, I fancy.'

' I know of a Madame Bâlo—B-â-l-o—who might answer to that description,' said the leader, thoughtfully, 'an elderly lady, a very fine pianiste. She still receives a few pupils—chiefly girls studying for concert playing; but I believe she does so more from love of her art than from any necessity to earn money. She lives in considerable comfort, and appears to be very well off.'

'She is a foreigner, I suppose, from the name. The lady I mean is—or was—an Englishwoman.

'Madame Bâlo is as British as you are. She may have married a foreigner, perhaps. But I really don't know whether she is a widow or a spinster. She lives alone, in a nice little house in Maida Vale.

' I wonder whether she can be the lady I want to find ? The description seems to answer. She may have Italianized the spelling of her name to make it more attractive to her patrons.'

'Yes, you English seem to have a small belief in your own musical abilities, since you prefer to entrust the cultivation of them to a foreigner.'

'Do you know this lady well enough to give me a note of introduction to her?' asked Maurice; 'if I may venture to ask such a favour at the beginning of our acquaintance.'

'Delighted to oblige a friend of Miss Elgood's,' answered Mr. Fisfiz, politely. 'Yes, I know Madame Bâlo well enough to scribble a note of introduction to her. She is a very clever woman, with a passion for clever people. And I believe you belong to the world of letters, Mr. Clissold?'

'Yes, I have dabbled in literature,' answered Maurice.

'Just the very man to delight Madame Bâlo. She is a woman of mind. When do you want the letter?'

'As soon as ever you can oblige me with it. I dare say a line on one of your cards would do as well. I merely wish to ask Madame Bâlo a few questions about a young lady who was once a member of her establishment at Seacomb ; supposingthat she is identical with the Miss Barlow I have spoken of.'

' I'll do what you want at once,' said Mr. Fisfiz.

He seated himself at the prompter's table, and wrote on the back of a card, in a neat and minute penmanship,—

' DEAR MADAME,—Mr. Clissold, the bearer of this card, is a literary gentleman of some standing, who wishes to make your acquaintance. Any favour you may accord him will also oblige,

' Yours very truly,

'R. F.'

' I think that will be quite enough for Madame Bâlo,' he said.

Half an hour later Maurice was in a hansom, bowling along the Edgware Road towards Maida Vale.

Here, on the banks of the canal, in a somewhat retired and even picturesque spot, he found the abode of Madame Bâlo, stuccoed and classical as to its external aspect, with a Corinthian portico, which almost extinguished the house to which it belonged.

A neat maid-servant opened the iron gate of the small parterre in front of the portico, and admitted him without question. She ushered him into a drawing-room handsomely furnished, and much ornamented with divers specimens of feminine handicraft—water-colour landscapes on the walls ; Berlin-work chair covers ; a tapestry screen, whereon industrious hands had imitated Landseer's famous Bolton Abbey ; fluffy and beady mats on the tables and chiffoniers ; and alabaster baskets of wax fruit and flowers carefully preserved under glass shades.

A glance at these things told Maurice that he was on the track of the original Miss Barlow. Such a collection of fancy-work could only belong to a retired schoolmistress.

A grand piano, open, with a well-filled music-stand beside it, occupied an important position in the room. Early as it was in the autumn, a bright little fire burned in the shining steel grate.

Maurice had ample leisure to study the characteristics of the apartment before Madame Bâlo made her appearance; but after examining all the works of art, and roaming about the room somewhat impatiently for some time, he heard an approaching rustle of silk, and Madame Bâlo entered, splendid in black moire antique, profusely bugled and fringed, and a delicate structure of pink crape and watered ribbon, which no doubt was meant for a cap.

She was a smiling, pleasant-looking little woman, short and stout, with a somewhat rubicund visage, and a mellow voice, nothing prim or scholastic about her appearance, her distinguishing quality being rather friendliness and an easy geniality.

'Delighted to see any friend of Mr. Fisfiz,' she said, with a gushing little manner that had something fresh and youthful about it, in spite of her sixty years; not affected juvenility, but the real thing. 'Charming man, Mr. Fisfiz—one of the finest quartette players I know. We have some pleasant evenings here now and then, when his theatre is shut. I should be happy to see you at my little parties, Mr. Clissold, if you are fond of chamber music.'

'You are very kind. I should be pleased to make one of your audience, however limited my powers of appreciation might be. But my call to-day is on a matter of business rather than of pleasure, and I fear I am likely to bore you by asking a good many questions.'

'Not at all,' said Madame Bâlo, with a gracious wave of the pink structure.

'First and foremost, then, may I venture to ask if you always spelt your name as it is inscribed on the brass plate on your gate, or whether its present orthography—the circumflex accent included—is not rather fanciful than correct? Pray pardon any seeming impertinence in my inquiry. The lady I am in quest of was proprietress of a school at Seacomb, in Cornwall, eminently respected by all who knew her. It struck me that you might be that very Miss Barlow.'

The lady blushed, coughed dubiously, and after a little hesitation, answered frankly,—

'Upon my word, Mr. Clissold, I don't know why I should be ashamed of the matter,' she said, smiling. 'It is a free country, and we are always taught that

we may do as we like with our own. Now nothing
can be more one's own property than one's name.'

'Certainly not.'

'When I came back to England, after a length-
ened sojourn in romantic Italy—the dream of my
life through many a year of toil,—I found that I was
still too young, and of far too energetic a temperament to settle down to idleness and retirement. I
am speaking now of fifteen years ago. In Italy I
had cultivated and improved my powers as an instru-
mentalist, and I had made myself mistress of the
mellifluous language to which a Dante and a Tasso
have lent renown. In Italy I had been known as
the Signora Bâlo. Gradually I had fallen into the
way of writing my name as my Italian friends preferred to write it; and ultimately, when I established
myself in this modest dwelling, and issued my
circulars, I preferred to appeal to a patrician and
fashionable public under the Italianized name of
Bâlo, and with the prefix Madame.'

'Your explanation is perfect, Madame,' replied
Maurice, 'and I thank you sincerely for your can-
dour. And now may I inquire if you remember

among your pupils at Seacomb a young lady of the name of Trevanard ? '

Madame Bâlo looked agitated.

' Remember Muriel Trevanard !' she exclaimed. ' I do indeed remember her. She was my favourite pupil, a lovely girl, full of talent—a charming creature.'

' Have you any idea of her fate in after life ? '

' No,' returned the schoolmistress, with a troubled look. ' It ought to have been brilliant, but I fear it was a blighted life.'

' It was indeed,' said Maurice, and then, as briefly as he could, told Madame Bâlo the story of her pupil's after life.

Madame Bâlo heard him with undisguised agitation. A little cry of horrified surprise broke from her more than once during his narrative.

' Now, after considering this case from every point of view, I arrived at a certain conclusion,' said Maurice.

' And that was—— '

' That George Penwyn and Muriel Trevanard

were man and wife, and that you were aware of their marriage.'

It was some moments before Madame Bâlo recovered herself sufficiently to reply. She sat looking straight before her, with a troubled countenance, then suddenly rose, and walked up and down the room once or twice—made as if she would have spoken, yet was dumb—and then as suddenly sat down again.

'Mr. Clissold,' she said abruptly, after these various evidences of a perturbed spirit, 'you have made me a very miserable woman.'

'I am sorry to hear that, Madame Bâlo.'

'That poor ill-used girl—that martyred girl—condemned by her own mother—disgraced and exiled in her own home—tortured till her brain gave way—was as honest a woman as I am—a true and loyal wife, bound to George Penwyn legally and with my knowledge. Yes, there was a marriage, and I was present at the ceremony. I foolishly permitted myself to be drawn into Captain Penwyn's boyish scheme of a secret marriage. It was to be the mere legal marriage, only a tie to bind them for ever—but no more than a tie until George should have won his father's consent, or been released by his father's death, and they should be free to complete their union. A foolish business, you will say, in the bud, but I was a foolish woman, and I thought it such a grand thing for my pet pupil—my bright and beautiful Muriel, whom I loved as if she had been my own daughter—to win the young Squire of Penwyn.'

Madame Bâlo said all this in little half-incoherent gushes, not strictly calculated to make things clear.

'If you would kindly give me a direct and succinct account of this matter—so far as you were concerned in it or privy to it—you would be doing me an extreme kindness, Madame Bâlo,' said Maurice, earnestly. 'Much wrong has been done that can never be repaired upon this earth ; but there is some part of the wrong that may perhaps be set right, if you will give me your uttermost aid.'

'It is yours, Mr. Clissold. Command me. You have no idea how fond I was of that poor girl—

how proud of the talents which it had been my privilege to develop.'

'Tell me everything ; straightly, simply, fully.'

'I will,' replied Madame Bâlo, 'and if I appear to blame in this unhappy story, you must remember I erred from want of thought. I believed that I was acting for the best.'

'Most of our mistakes in this life are made under that delusion,' said Maurice, with his grave smile.

'You want to know how I came to be mixed up in Muriel's love affair ? First you must know that before he went to Eton, George Penwyn came to me to be prepared for a public school. I was a mere girl, and had only just set up my establishment for young ladies in those days, and I was very glad to give two hours every morning to the Squire's little boy, who used to ride over to Seacomb on his Exmoor pony in the charge of a groom. A very dear little fellow he was at nine years old. I grounded him in French and Latin—and even taught him the rudiments of Greek during the year and a half in which I had him for a pupil, my

own dear father having given me a thorough classical education : and, without vanity, I do not think
many little lads went to Eton that year better
prepared than George Penwyn. He was a grateful,
warm-hearted boy, and he never forgot his old
friend, or the old-fashioned garden with the big
yellow egg-plums on the western wall. He came to
see me many a time in his summer holidays, and
afterwards when he was in the army. I never
knew him to be three days at home without spending a morning with me. He was about the only
young man I ever let come in and out of my house
without restraint, for I knew he was the soul
of honour.'

'Did he first see Muriel Trevanard in your
house ? '

' No, he was abroad at the time Muriel was with
me. My first knowledge of his acquaintance with
Muriel, and of his love for her, came from his own
lips, and came to me as a surprise.'

Madame Bâlo paused, with a sigh, and then
continued her story.

'Captain Penwyn came to me one day, just before

the Michaelmas holidays—it was about a year after
Muriel had gone home for good—and asked me for
half an hour's private talk. Well do I remember that
calm September afternoon, and his bright, eager face
as he walked up and down together in the garden at
Seacomb, by the sunny wall, where the last of the
figs and plums were ripening. He told me he was
madly in love with Muriel Trevanard—deeper in
love than he had ever been in his life—in fact, it
was the one true passion of his life. "I may have
fancied myself in love before," he said, "but this is
reality." I tried to laugh him out of his fancy,
reminded him of the difference in station between
himself and a tenant farmer's daughter ; asked him
what his father would say to such an infatuation.
"That's what I'm here to talk about," said George.
"You know what my father is, and that I might just
as well try to turn the course of those two rivers we
used to read about when you were grinding me as
to turn my father from his purpose. He has made
up his mind that I am to marry land—he dreams of
land, sleeping and waking—and spends half his
time in calculating the number of his acres. If I

refuse to marry land he will disinherit me, and one of my younger brothers will get Penwyn. Now you know how fond I am of Penwyn, and how fond all the people round Penwyn are of me; and you may imagine that it would be rather a hard blow for me to lose an estate which I have always looked upon as my birthright."

'" I should think so, indeed," said I.

'" But I love Muriel Trevanard better than house or land," replied he, "and I would rather lose all than lose her." '

' What did you say to this ? ' asked Maurice.

' I told him that he was simply mad to think about Muriel, except as he might of a beautiful picture which he had seen in a gallery. But I might as well have reasoned with the wind. He had made up his mind that life without Muriel wasn't worth having. If ever I saw passionate, reckless, all-absorbing love in my life, I saw it in him. Nothing would content him but that Muriel and he should be married before he went abroad with his regiment. He only wanted the tie, the certainty that nothing less than death could part

them. He would ask no more than that she should
be legally his wife, and would wait a fitting time to
take her away from her father's house, and proclaim
his marriage to the world. Nothing would be
gained by my repeating the arguments I used.
They were of no avail. He held to his foolish
romantic purpose of calling Muriel his wife before he
left England. "I shall only be away a year or two,"
he said, "and who knows but I may gain a shred of
reputation before I come back—return full major,
perhaps, and be able to soften my father's flinty
heart?" He told me that he wanted my help, but if
I refused it the marriage would take place all the
same. He would not leave England until he had
made Muriel his own.'

'And you consented to help him?'

'He talked me out of my better reason. Mr.
Clissold, I must confess to a romantic temperament,
and that reason is not my strong point. I was
touched by the intensity of his love—the romance
of the situation—and after a long argument, and
doing my uttermost to dissuade George from the
step he contemplated, I ultimately promised him

my aid—and pledged myself to the strictest secrecy. Muriel was to be asked to spend the Michaelmas holidays with me, and then we were to go quietly to a little watering-place in Devonshire, where no one would know anything about us, or about George Penwyn. George was to slip up to Exeter for the licence, and everything was to be managed in such a way as to prevent the possibility of suspicion on the part of the Squire.'

'Did Muriel consent readily to such a plan?'

'I think not. But, however unwillingly, her consent had been given before she came to me, and when I, as woman to woman, asked her if she really wished this marriage to take place she told me yes, she wished all that George wished. He had a foolish idea that her father and mother would oblige her to marry some one else if he left her unfettered, she told me, and nothing would satisfy him but that indissoluble bond. Well, we went to Didmouth, the quietest little seaport town you can well imagine, and here Muriel and I lived in lodgings, while George had his quarters at the hotel. I think those were happy days for both of them. The country round Didmouth is lovely, and they used to wander about together all day long on the hills, and in the lanes where the blackberries were ripening, and the ferns beginning to change their tint. I never saw such innocent, happy lovers. The simplest things pleased and interested them. They were full of hope for the future, when the old Squire should relent. I don't know how they supposed he would be brought to change his ideas, but they had some vague notion that he would come round to George's way of thinking in a year or two. As the wedding day drew near their spirits drooped a little, for it was an understood thing that they were to part at the church door, and meet no more until the Squire's consent had been won, lest, by any imprudent meeting, they should betray the secret of their union, and bring about George's disinheritance. I made them both promise most solemnly that they would not meet after the wedding until George had told his father all, and settled his future fate for good or evil. I stood beside Muriel at the altar; I signed my name in the parish register. I saw bride and bridegroom kiss with their parting kiss, and then I took my old pupil off to the Didmouth coach—there was no rail to Didmouth in those days—and by nightfall we were back in Seacomb, worn out both of us with the emotions of that curious wedding day. A few days later Muriel went back to Borcel End, and I saw no more of her till the following Christmas, when I drove over to the farm one afternoon to say good-bye to my old pupil, after having advantageously disposed of my school in rather a sudden way, and on the eve of my departure for the Continent. I could only see Muriel in the presence of her mother and father, who received me with old-fashioned ceremoniousness, and gave me no opportunity of being alone with my pupil. And thus I left Cornwall ignorant of any need that Muriel might have of my friendship, counsel, or aid. I looked upon George Penwyn's marriage as the foolish whim of a headstrong young man, passionately in love; but I had no thought that peril or ruin could come of that act; and I looked forward hopefully to the time when Captain Penwyn would return and claim his wife before all the world. Whether the old Squire did or did not forego his threat of an unjust will, it would be no bad thing for Muriel to be a captain's or a major's wife, I thought, even if her husband were landless, or fortuneless. Better than marrying trade or agriculture, I told myself. Very foolish, no doubt; but my dear old father, who taught me the classics, taught me a good many prejudices into the bargain, and though I had to get my living as a schoolmistress, I always looked down upon trade. It pleased me to think that the girl, whose mind I had formed, had a gentleman for her husband, and a gentleman descended from one of the oldest families in Cornwall. And now, Mr. Clissold, that is the whole of my story. From the time I left Seacomb I never heard from Muriel Penwyn, though I had given her my London agent's address when we parted, an address from which letters would always be forwarded to me.'

'You heard of her husband's death, I suppose?'

'Not till nearly six months after it happened, when I saw an account of the poor fellow's melancholy fate in an Italian newspaper, a paragraph copied from *Galignani*. You may imagine that my heart bled for Muriel, yet I dared not write to express my sympathy, fearing to betray a secret which she might prefer to keep hidden for ever from her parents. The foolish marriage was now no more than a dream, I thought; a shadow which had passed across the sunshine of her bright young life, leaving grief and pain in its track, but exercising no serious influence on her future. "She will get over her sorrow in a year or so, and marry some good-looking farmer, or Seacomb shopkeeper, after all,' I thought, bitterly disappointed at this sad ending to my pretty little romance. I wrote to a friend at Seacomb soon after to inquire about my old pupil, putting my questions with assumed carelessness. My friend replied that Miss Trevanard was still unmarried and with her parents—a dull life for the poor girl, she feared,—but she understood that Miss Trevanard was well. This was all I could hear.'

'The breaking of a heart is a quiet transaction,' said Maurice, 'hardly noticeable to the outward world. Small-pox is a far more obvious calamity.'

Madame Bâlo sighed. She felt that she had some cause for remorse on the subject of Muriel

Trevanard, that she had taken too little trouble about the young wife's after fate—had been too much absorbed by her own musical studies, her Continental friends and her own interests generally

'What was the name of the church at Didmouth where the marriage took place?' asked Maurice.

'The parish church, St. John's.'

'And the date of the marriage?'

'September 30th, 1847.'

This was all th at Madame Bâlo could tell him and all that he wanted to know. It seemed to him that his course was tolerably clear. He had three distinct facts to prove. First the marriage, then the birth of the infant, and finally Justina's identity with that infant.

His three witnesses would be—

1. Miss Barlow, to prove the marriage.

2. Old Mrs. Trevanard, who could testify to the birth of the child.

3. Matthew Elgood, in whose custody Justina had been from the day of her birth, and whose evidence, if held worthy of credence,

must needs establish her identity with the child born at Borcel End.

On leaving Madame Bâlo, with whom he parted on excellent terms, Maurice went straight to his solicitors, Messrs. Willgross and Harding, of Old Square, good old family solicitors,—substantial, reliable, sagacious. Before the younger partner, his especial friend and counsellor, he laid his case.

Mr. Harding heard him with a thoughtful countenance, and was in no haste to commit himself to an opinion.

'Rather difficult to dispossess such a man as this Mr. Churchill Penwyn, on the testimony of a strolling player,' he said. 'It's a pity you haven't witnesses with better standing in the world. It might look like a got-up case.'

'There is the evidence of the parish register at Didmouth Church.'

'To prove the marriage. Yes; but only an old blind woman to prove the birth of an heiress, and only this Elgood to show that the infant was entrusted to him. And on the strength of his evidence you want to claim an estate worth seven

thousand a year for a young actress at the Albert
Theatre. The story is very pretty, very romantic,
but, upon my word, Mr. Clissold, between friends,
if I were you, I would not take much trouble
about it.'

'I will take whatever trouble may be needful to
prove Justina's legitimacy,' replied Maurice, with
decision. 'The estate is a secondary consideration.'

'Of course, a mere bagatelle. Well, one of our
clerks shall go down to Didmouth to make a copy of
the entry in the register.'

'I'll go with him,' said Maurice.

CHAPTER X.

MAURICE left London for Didmouth by the mail, accompanied by Mr. Pointer, a confidential clerk of Messrs. Willgross and Harding. Didmouth was still off the main line, and they had to drive seven or eight miles in a jolting little omnibus, very low in the roof, and by no means luxurious within. They reached Didmouth too late for anything except supper and bed, but they were at the sexton's cottage before eight o'clock next morning, and thence repaired to the church, with the elderly custodian and his keys in their company.

The registers were produced, and the entry of the marriage found, under the date supplied by Miss Barlow. A duly certified copy of this entry being taken by Mr. Pointer, in duplicate, Maurice's mission at Didmouth was concluded.

He parted from Mr. Pointer at the railway station, after having endured another hour of the jolting omnibus ; and while the clerk hastened back to London with one of the two documents, Maurice went down the line to Seacomb with the other.

He had not been away a week, and yet he had established the one fact he most desired to prove, Justina's right to bear her father's name. He could now venture to confide Muriel's story to Martin, or at least so much of it as might be told without reflecting on his dead mother.

He walked into the old farmhouse at breakfast-time next morning, after having spent the night at Seacomb, and crossed the moors in the autumnal mists of earliest morning, not without some hazard of losing his way.

Martin was surprised and delighted.

'What good wind blows you here, dear old fellow ? ' he cried, gladly.

'The best wind that ever blew, I think, answered Maurice.

Mr. Trevanard had gone about his day's work, he had taken to working harder than ever, of late,

Martin said ; so the two young men had the old hall to themselves.

Here Maurice told his story, Martin listening with profound emotion, and shedding no unmanly **tears** at the record of his sister's sorrows.

'**My poor mother**!' he sobbed out at **last**. 'She acted for **the** best—to save the honour of our family —but it was hard on Muriel—and she was sinless all the **time—a wife,** free from taint of **wrong-doing,** except **that** fatal concealment of her **marriage.'**

Then, when the first shock was over, **the young** man inquired eagerly about his niece, his beloved sister's **only child**—the babe that had been exiled from its birthplace, robbed of its name.

'**How** nobly, how wisely, how ably you have acted from **first** to last, Clissold!' he exclaimed, 'Without your help this tangled web could never have been unravelled. But how did it ever occur to you that Miss Elgood and my sister's daughter could be one and the same person?'

'Perhaps it was because I have thought so much more of Justina Elgood lately than any one else,'

answered Maurice ; and then he went on to confess
that his old wound was healed, and that he loved
Justina with a deeper and truer love than he had
given the doctor's daughter. Martin was delighted.
This would make a new link between himself and
his friend.

Maurice's next anxiety was for an interview with
old Mrs. Trevanard. He wanted to test that aged
memory, to discover how far the blind grandmother might be relied upon when the time came
for laying this family secret before the world.

Mrs. Trevanard still kept her room. She was
able to move about a little—able to keep watch and
ward upon Muriel, but she preferred the retirement
of her own chamber to her old corner in the family
sitting-room.

'The place would seem strange to me without
Bridget,' she told Maurice, when he expressed his
regret at finding her still in her own room. 'It's
not so much the rheumatics that keep me here as the
thought of that. Bridget was all in all in this house.
The old room would seem desolate without her. So
I just keep by my own bit of fire, and knit my stock-
ing, and think of old times.'

' I dare say your memory is a better one than many young people can boast of,' said Maurice, who had taken the empty chair by the fireplace, opposite Mrs. Trevanard.

'Well, I haven't much to complain of in that respect,' answered the old woman, with a sigh. ' I have sometimes thought that it is better for old people when their memories are not quite so strong as mine. But then, perhaps, that's owing to my blindness. I have nothing left me but memory, I can't see to read, not even my Bible, and I haven't many about me that care to read to me. So the past is my book, and I'm always reading the saddest chapters in it. It's a pity Providence has made us so that our minds dwell longest on sorrowful things."

Maurice related his discovery gently and with some preparation to Muriel's grandmother. When she heard that Muriel was sinless, that her marriage with George Penwyn was an established fact, the blind woman lifted up her voice in thanksgiving to her God.

' I always thought as much,' she said, after that

first outpouring of prayer and praise. 'I always thought my poor lamb was innocent, but Bridget would not have it so. Bridget hugged the notion of our wrong. She was always talking of God's vengeance on the wrong-doer, and when he met with that cruel death she declared that it was a judgment, forgetting that the judgment fell heaviest on our poor Muriel.'

They talked long and earnestly of the hapless daughter of the house, Maurice confiding unreservedly in Mrs. Trevanard, who evinced a shrewd sense that filled him with hope. Old and blind though she was, this was not a witness to be browbeaten by a cross-examining counsel, should the issue ever be tried in a court of justice.

'Now from what we know, and from what happened to me on the first night I ever spent in this house,' said Maurice, 'it is clear to my mind that your granddaughter and her husband were in the habit of meeting secretly in the room at the end of the corridor at night, when every one else in the house was asleep.'

He went on to describe his first night at Borcel

End; Muriel watching at the open window, entreating her lover to come back to her. Did not this conduct indicate that Captain Penwyn had been in the habit of entering the house secretly by that window? Its height was little over eight feet from the ground, and the ivy-clad wall would have been easy enough for any active young man to climb, to say nothing of the ledge and projecting masonry of the low window, which made the ascent still easier.

'My idea is this,' said Maurice. 'Your poor granddaughter's instinct takes her to that room whenever she is free to ramble about the house at night when all is still, and she has no fear of interruption. For her that room is haunted by sad and sweet memories. What more likely than that if free to go there nightly she would, in the self-communion of a wandering mind, reveal more of the past than we have yet learned, act over again her meetings with her lover, say over again the old words? Will you leave her free to wander to-night, if the fancy seizes her? I will lie down in my clothes, and keep watch, ready to listen, or to follow her if need be.

The moon is nearly at the full, and the night will be bright enough to tempt her to wander. Will you let it be so, Mrs. Trevanard?'

'I don't see that any harm could come of it,' answered the old woman, dubiously. 'She is reasonable enough in her way, and I have never known her attempt to do herself a mischief. But as to what she can reveal in her wild wandering talk, I don't see myself how that can be of any good.'

'Perhaps not. It is only a fancy of mine at best, but I shall be pleased if you will indulge it. I shall not be here more than two or three nights.'

'I will leave my door unlocked on those nights,' said Mrs. Trevanard. 'But I shall not have much rest while that poor child is wandering about.'

To the grandmother, to whom the past was more real than the present, Muriel was still the girl of eighteen newly returned from school.

The rest of the day was spent quietly enough by Maurice and Martin in a ramble on the sea-shore. At dinner Mr. Trevanard appeared, but although he was surprised to see Maurice so soon after his departure he evinced no curiosity as to the motive of his return. The master of Borcel farm seemed to have lost all interest in life in losing the partner of his joys and cares. He went about his work with a mechanical air, talked very little, drank more than he eat, and seemed altogether in a bad way

Maurice observed him with concern.

'If we could but kindle a glimmer of reason in his daughter's breast, she might be a comfort to him in the decline of his life,' speculated the poet, 'and it is just possible that a father's love might exercise some healing influence upon that disordered mind. The isolation to which her mother condemned her was the surest method of deadening mind and memory.'

He would have given much had he been free to summon Justina to Borcel, and test the power of a daughter's love upon Muriel's brain. But to bring Justina away from London would be to imperil the prosperity of the Albert Theatre, and doubtless to incur onerous legal penalties. Nor did he wish to draw Justina into the business till his chain of evidence was too complete for the possibility of failure in the establishment of her rights.

'No,' he told himself, 'for some time to come I must act without Justina.'

Martin could talk of nothing but his newly discovered niece, and was full of impatience to see her. It was only by promising to take him to London in a few days, and introduce him to Justina, that Maurice succeeded in keeping this young man quiet during his first day at Borcel End. And thus the day wore itself out, and night, with the full autumn moonlight, descended upon the old farmhouse,

CHAPTER XI.

It was a clear autumn night, still and cloudless.
The mists of evening had rolled away from moorland and meadow,—from the dark brown fields
where the plough had been busy, and the long
line of rippling water. The moon was as bright
and full as on that first night of Maurice Clissold's
sojourn at Borcel. He had been told that on such a
night as this Muriel was wont to be restless.

'Now if that poor ghost of days departed will
but haunt my room to-night, I may gather some
shred of information from her disjointed talk,' he
said to himself.

But the night wore away while he lay awake and
watchful, and there was no sound of slippered footfall in the corridor, no opening of the creaking old
door. Mr. Clissold fell asleep at last, when the

moon had vanished, and did not wake till ever so long after the Borcel End breakfast-hour.

This was disappointing, but he waited another day, and watched another night, with the same result.

'If she doesn't come to-night I give it up, he said to himself. 'After all, there can be but little for me to gather from her rambling self-communion.'

He slept for an hour or two on the third afternoon, and thus on the third night of his watch was more wakeful than before. The nights were moonlight still, but the moon rose later, and had lost her full brightness.

He lay awake for three hours on this particular night, and heard not a sound, save the occasional scufflings, patterings, and squealings of mice behind the wainscot. But a few minutes after the eight-day clock in the hall had struck two, the watcher heard the sound that had startled him at his first coming—the slipshod footfall—the slow, ghost-like tread on the uncarpeted floor of the corridor.

Muriel was approaching.

She entered slowly—quietly—as before, and went straight to the window, which she opened noiselessly, taking infinite pains to avoid all sound. Then, kneeling on the window-seat, she put her head out of the window, and looked downward, as if she were watching some one below.

' Be careful, love,' she exclaimed, in a whisper just loud enough to reach Maurice's attentive ear, ' that root of ivy is loose.   I'm afraid your foot will slip.   Be careful!'

For some time she remained thus, holding imaginary communion with some one below.   Then all at once she awoke to a sense of her solitude, and knew that she had been talking to a phantom.   She drew back into the room, and began to walk up and down rapidly, with a distracted air, her hands clasped upon her head, as if by that pressure upon her temples she would have stilled the trouble within her brain.

' They told me he was dead,' she said to herself; ' murdered, barbarously murdered.   But there was no truth in it.'   They have told me other lies as well as that.   They are all false, all cruel.   My mother has made them so. She has taken away my husband. She has taken away my child. She has left me nothing but memory. Why did she not take that away? I should be happy—yes, quite happy, sitting by the fire and singing all day long, or roaming about among the hazel bushes, and the old apple-trees in the wilderness, if I did not remember. But I look down at my empty arms and remember that my blessed child ought to be lying in them, and then I hate her. Yes, I hate the mother that bore me.'

All this was said in disjointed gushes of quick, eager speech, divided by intervals of silence.

Suddenly she burst into a shrill laugh.

'Who says he is dead?' she cried. 'Don't I see him every moonlight night when I can come here? They shut me up mostly, lock all their doors, and keep me prisoner. Cruel—cruel—cruel. But he is standing under the window all the same, when-ever the moon shines. He is there, waiting for me to open my window, like Romeo. Yes, that's what he said, " like Romeo." '

Then with an entire change of tone, a change to

deepest **tenderness,** mingled with **a** remorseful fear, she **went on,** as if speaking **to her** lover.

'**Love,** it was very **wrong of** us to break our promise. I fear that **harm** will come of it. **My mind** is full **of fear.'**

After this came **a** long silence. She went back to the window, **knelt** upon the broad wooden seat laid her **head upon** the sill, **and remained motionless,** speechless.

Maurice fancied she was weeping.

This continued for nearly **an hour; then with a** sudden movement—all her movements were sudden —she started up **and** looked **about** the room, as if in quest of something.

Maurice **had** left his extinguished candle **on** the dressing-table, **with a box of** matches **in the** candlestick. Quick as thought, Muriel seized the box, **struck a** match, and lighted **the candle, and** then hurried from the room.

The watcher sprang **from the bed** where he had been lying hidden by the shadow of the curtains, and followed that retiring figure, full of apprehen- **sion.**

A confirmed lunatic rushing about an old timber house with a lighted candle was not the safest of people, and Maurice held himself responsible for any harm that might happen in consequence of Muriel's liberty.

When he emerged from his room the corridor was empty, but the gleam of the candle in the distance guided his hurried steps. At the end of the corridor there was a winding stair—a stair which he had 'never ascended—but which he understood to lead to certain disused garrets in the roof.

It was from this narrow stair that the light came, and hither Maurice hastened. He was just in time to see the edge of Muriel's white drapery flutter for an instant on the topmost stair before it vanished, and the light with it.

He rushed up the stairs, knocking his head against a heavy cross-beam in the course of his swift ascent, and almost stunning himself; but even that blow did not make him pause. He staggered on to the last step, and found himself in a kind of cavern, which in the dim light of the waning moon looked to him like the hold of a ship turned upside

down.   Ponderous beams crossed each other in every
direction—the faint moonshine streamed through a
broken skylight—cobwebs and dust hung all around,
and in one corner of this deserted loft a few articles
of furniture were crowded together, shrouded from
the dust by some old patchwork coverlets.   Even
this loft had doubtless been kept in good order so
long as that vigilant housewife, Bridget Trevanard
had been able to attend to her domestic duties.

Muriel was kneeling near this shrouded heap of
discarded furniture—kneeling by an old-fashioned
basket-work cradle. She held the candlestick in
one hand, and seemed to be searching for something
in the cradle with the other hand. Her head was
bent, her brow contracted, and she was muttering to
herself as she groped among the tumbled blankets
and discoloured linen which had once made the
warm nest of some idolized infant. Her own nest,
most likely.

Maurice stopped short. To startle her in such a
moment might be dangerous. Better for him to hold
his peace, and keep a watch upon her movements,
ready to rush to the rescue, should there be peril.

Presently she seemed to have found what she
wanted. It was a letter, in a sealed envelope, which
she looked at and kissed, but made no attempt to
open. She replaced this presently in the cradle, and
took out more letters, two or three together, open,
and these she kissed, looking long and fixedly at the
written lines, as if she were trying to read them, but
could not.

'My love, my love,' she murmured. 'Your own
true words—nothing but death could part us. Death
has parted us. Yes, death! They told me you
were dead. And yet that can't be true. The dead
are spirits. If you were dead you would hover
near me. I should see your blessed shade. I
should——'

Her eyes, wandering slowly from the letter,
penetrated that dusky corner where Maurice stood
watching her. She saw him—gave one long, wild
shriek—and sprang towards him.

To her excited imagination that dark and silent
form seemed the ghost of her dead lover.

She had thrown the candlestick from her as she
sprang to her feet. The candle rolled from its

socket and fell upon her long night-dress. A moment, and she stood before Maurice's affrighted sight a pillar of flame.

He flew to her, clasped her in his arms, and trampled on the candle, dragged one of the loose coverings from the furniture, and rolled her in it tightly, firmly, extinguishing the flames in his vigorous grasp. The peril, the horror, had been but momentary, yet he feared the shock might be fatal. The frail form shivered in his arms. The tender flesh had been scorched.

Even in that moment of terror she still believed him to be her lover.

'Not a spirit!' she murmured. 'Not the shadow of the dead, but living, and returned to me, to rescue, to cherish! Oh, George, is it really you?'

It was the first time he had heard her utter George Penwyn's name.

'It is one who will protect and cherish you,' Maurice said, tenderly. 'One whom you may trust and cling to in all confidence, one who will restore your daughter to you.'

'My daughter, my baby girl!' she cried. 'No?

you can never do that on earth; in heaven we shall meet again, perhaps, and know each other, but never in this life. She was taken away from me, and they murdered her.'

'No; she was given into safe hands, she was loved and cared for. Years have passed since then, and she has grown up into a beautiful young woman. You shall see her again, live with her, and she will love and honour you.'

'I don't want her, I want my lovely baby, the little child they took away from me. The baby that lay in my arms, and clung to my breast for one short hour before it was taken away.'

She shuddered, and a faint moan broke from her lips.

'You are in pain,' said Maurice.

'Yes, the fire is burning still. It scorches me to the heart.'

He took her up in his arms with infinite tenderness, and carried her across the loft, and down the narrow stair, making his way amidst those massive cross-beams, and by those steep steps with extreme caution, lighted only by the pale glimmer of a fading moon.

Once at the bottom of the stairs, and in the broad corridor, his way was easy enough. He carried his light burden through the silent house, across the empty hall, to old Mrs. Trevanard's room. Here he laid her gently on the sofa before awaking the blind grandmother. He found a candle on the table, and a match-box on the mantelpiece, and was soon provided with a light.

His first look was at Muriel. She had fainted, and lay motionless where he had placed her—white and death-like.

He went to Mrs. Trevanard's bedside, and woke her gently.

'Dear Mrs. Trevanard, there has been an accident. Your granddaughter is hurt; not seriously, I trust, but the shock has made her faint. Will you give her some kind of restorative, while I go and call the servants?'

He left the room for this purpose, hurried to the end of the house where he had been told the servants slept, in a room over the kitchen, knocked at the door of this room, and told one of the girls to get up and dress herself as fast as she could, and come to

Mrs. Trevanard's room without a moment's loss of time. This done, he hastened back to Muriel, and found the blind grandmother administering to her—holding a glass containing some cordial of her own concoction to the white lips of the sufferer.

'Why did you persuade me to leave my door open?' exclaimed Mrs. Trevanard, reproachfully. 'See what harm has come of it.'

'Not much harm, I trust in Providence. There has been a shock, but I hope no real injury.'

'What was it? Did she fall?'

'No, it was worse than a fall.'

He told how the flame had caught Muriel's thin night-gear, and how rapidly it had been extinguished.

'If you will tell me where to find your doctor, I will saddle one of the farm horses and ride over to fetch him, however far it may be,' said Maurice.

'*You* ride!' cried Mrs. Trevanard, contemptuously, 'and how are you to find your way from here to Seacomb before daybreak?'

'I am not afraid. I have driven the road often with Martin.'

'Let Martin go. He has known the way from childhood.'

This seemed a reasonable suggestion, and Maurice hurried off to wake Martin, just as Phœbe the housemaid arrived on the scene, sleepy, but sympathetic. She had expected to find old Mrs. Trevanard ill; in fact, had made up her mind that the old lady had had 'a stroke,' and was at her last gasp. She was therefore surprised to find the blind woman keen and active, only needing the aid of some one with eyes, to carry out her instructions.

Maurice was not sorry to remain on the spot while Martin went for the doctor, feeling that coolness and nerve might be needful.

Martin was up and dressed in the briefest possible space of time, and ran out to the stables to saddle the useful hack which was kept for the dog-cart. Day was beginning to show faint and pale in the east as he galloped away by the road that led to Seacomb, the same road by which Matthew Elgood and his wife had gone in the chill March morning, twenty years before, with Muriel's child in their custody.

Maurice walked up and down the hall, listening for any sound from that inner room, and in half an hour had the satisfaction of hearing that she was sleeping tranquilly, and that she had been very little burned.

'Thank God!' he ejaculated fervently. 'If this accident had been fatal I should have deemed myself her murderer.'

At seven o'clock the doctor arrived, an old man with a wise, kind face. He had assisted at Muriel's birth, and had been in some measure familiar with the various stages of her life, though never entrusted with the fatal family secret.

He made light of the accident.

'A shock to the system, undoubtedly,' he said, 'but I trust not involving any danger. Indeed, I am not without hope that it may have a beneficial effect in subduing that restlessness which Mrs. Trevanard tells me is the worst feature of the case. Anything which would induce repose would be favourable, and, by and by, perhaps, change of air and scene—a total change of surroundings— might do good in weaning the mind from old impressions, introducing, if I may say so, a new colour into the patient's life. I have often suggested this to our worthy friend the late Mrs. Trevanard, but without effect. She had her prejudices, good soul, and she thought her daughter could only be properly cared for at home.'

'And do you think your patient might soon be moved?' asked Maurice, who had a scheme for bringing mother and daughter together.

'Well, not immediately. Under present circumstances rest is most to be desired, but when strength returns I feel assured that change would be advantageous.'

When he had heard all the doctor had to say and eaten a hasty breakfast, Maurice went quietly upstairs, and having reconnoitred the corridor, and assured himself that there was nobody about to watch his movements, ascended that upper staircase leading to the loft.

It was broad daylight now in that chaotic cavern formed by the roof of the old house. The sunshine streamed in through the broken skylight, revealing every cobweb which festooned the old oak rafters. Maurice stepped cautiously across the creaking timbers which roughly floored the chamber, and approached the pile of disused furniture, in front of which stood the little wicker cradle where Muriel had hidden her letters.

Were they actual letters, Maurice wondered, or only scraps of worthless paper which her distraught fancy had invested with meaning and importance? Had she hidden her lover's letters here in the days when her mind was bright and clear, or had she strayed hither in the cunning of madness, to secrete the maniac's treasures of straws and shreds and discarded scraps of paper? He knelt beside the cradle as she had knelt, and turned out the little sheets and blankets, the small down pillows. Yes; there were letters under the mattress, a small packet of letters written in rusty ink on discoloured paper, tied with a faded ribbon.

'These may be worth something in the way of evidence,' he said to himself.

He read them one after another as he knelt there. They told the old story of deathless love doomed to die, of bright hopes never to blossom into reality. They all began 'My beloved wife,' they were all signed 'Your devoted husband,

George Penwyn.' They were all addressed on the cover, which was an integral part of each letter, 'Miss Muriel Trevanard, Borcel End, near Seacomb.'

There could be no doubt as to the identity of the person to whom the letters had been written. There could be no doubt as to the writer's recognition of that person as his lawful wife. 'My Muriel, my darling wife,' occurred many times in the letters. Nor was this all—in these letters, written in all love and confidence, George Penwyn made frequent allusion to the motives which had led to his secret marriage. His whole mind was here laid bare, his hope of the Squire's relenting in time to come, his plans for the future, his intention to declare his marriage at any hazard, immediately upon his return to England, his willingness to face poverty, if need were, with Muriel.

' But I am not without the hope,' he wrote in one of the later letters, ' that my absence from England for two or three years will have a good effect upon my father's feelings towards me. He is sore now on account of my having neglected what he was pleased to consider a grand opportunity of enlarging and consolidating the Penwyn Estate. But I know that in his heart he loves me best of all his sons, and that it would lacerate that heart to disinherit me. Time will blunt the edge of his angry feelings, and when I come back, perhaps with some little distinction as a soldier, he will be inclined to look leniently upon my choice.'

In another letter he hinted at the possible arising of circumstances which would oblige Muriel to leave her home.

'I could not go away without being assured that you have a friend and counsellor ready to aid you in any difficulty,' he wrote. 'I have a staunch friend in Mr. Tomlin, the lawyer, of Seacomb, and I herewith enclose a letter which I have written to him, informing him of our marriage, and enlisting his sympathy and assistance for you, should you need them. He will do all that friendship and discretion can inspire, both to secure your comfort and happiness, your safety and respectability of surroundings *under all circumstances*, and also to assure the preservation of our secret. Give your mind no trouble, darling, whatever may happen, but trust implicitly in Mr. Tomlin's wisdom and kindness, and believe that, distant as I may be in the body, there is no hour of the day or night in which I am not near you in the spirit.'

The letter, addressed to William Tomlin, Esq., Solicitor, Seacomb, was here—the seal unbroken.

Maurice had no doubt that the possible difficulty foreseen by the young husband before he left England, was the difficulty which had actually arisen in the birth of Justina. But why had this letter been left undelivered ? How came it that this unhappy wife —finding herself in the most miserable position a woman could be placed in—her honour doubted even by her own mother—should have refrained from applying to the friend and adviser to whom her husband had recommended her, and to whose allegiance he had confided her future ?

Had she deliberately chosen to endure unmerited disgrace in her own home, rather than avail herself of Mr. Tomlin's aid—or had her brain already begun to fail at the time when her trouble fell upon her, rendering her incapable of taking the most obvious as well as the most rational course?

This question sorely puzzled Maurice, and was for the time unanswerable. He put the letters in his breast pocket, feeling that with this documentary evidence to strengthen Justina's case, there must be little doubt as to the issue. The only question open to dispute in the face of the marriage register, and of these letters, would be the identity of Justina. He went downstairs, and out of the house, and took a long ramble across the upland fields, with the Atlantic before him —his favourite walk at all times, these bleak fields of turnip or mangold, high above the roaring waves and wild romantic coast, with its jagged peaks and natural arches and obelisks of serpentine.

There were a family of cormorants disporting themselves among the rocks—one solitary herring-boat bobbing up and down in the distance, a man shovelling up seaweed into a cart on the beach ; and this, save for the flash of a sea-gull's silver wing now and then, was all the life visible from the turnip-field on the cliff. Here Martin came presently, refreshed by a couple of hours' sleep after his long ride.

'I thought I should find you here,' he said, 'when I missed you in the house. Poor Muriel is going on very comfortably. I was with her just now when she awoke. She knew me, for a wonder, and was more gentle than I have found her for a long time, but the shock seems to have weakened her very much.'

'One could hardly expect it could be otherwise. A few days' rest will restore her, I trust. Believe me, Martin, no one could be more anxious about her than I.'

'I am sure of that, dear fellow.'

'And now answer me a question. Did you ever hear the name of Tomlin?'

'Yes, there is a solicitor of that name at Sea-comb.'

'An old man?'

'No, middle-aged, at most. I should think him barely forty.'

'Then he is not the man I want. He had a father before him, I suppose?'

'Yes, old Mr. Tomlin was a wonderful fellow, I believe, universally respected. I never saw him to my knowledge, for he died when I was a youngster, but I have often heard my father talk of him.'

Half an hour afterwards, when they were seated at the farmer's early dinner, Maurice took occasion to question Michael Trevanard on the same subject.

'Old Mr. Tomlin?' said the farmer. 'Yes, I remember him well, though he never did any business for me. A very worthy man, everybody liked him; a lawyer in a thousand, a thoroughly honest man. He died suddenly, poor fellow. Left his house one morning in excellent health to attend the petty sessions, and was seized with a stroke of apoplexy in the court and never spoke again. His funeral was one of the grandest I ever saw in Seacomb.'

'Do you happen to remember the year of his death?'

'Yes, I remember it well, for it occurred in the winter, before Muriel's long illness. He died in December, 1847. This explained Muriel's conduct. Death had snatched away the one friend to whom she could have made her appeal.

CHAPTER XII.

'IT IS TIME, O PASSIONATE HEART,' SAID I.

THE reason of Muriel's conduct was fully explained
by the fact of Mr. Tomlin's death. The one friend
whom her husband's forethought had provided for her
had been snatched away before the hour of her need,
and she had found herself alone, without help,
counsel, or shelter. Doubtless an overstrained
respect for her promise—perhaps a latent fear of
Bridget Trevanard's severe nature — had withheld
her from revealing the fact of her marriage and the
manner of it. She had borne the deep agony of shame
rather than endanger her husband's future. She had
perhaps argued that if her mother and father had
been told the truth, nothing would have prevented
their communicating it to the Squire, and then
George would have been disinherited through her

broken promise. Woman-like, she had deemed her own peace—her own fair fame even—a lighter sacrifice than her husband's welfare, and she had kept silence.

With this additional evidence of George Penwyn's letters, fully acknowledging Muriel as his wife, Maurice felt that there was no further cause for delay. The law could not be too soon set in motion, if the law were needed to secure Muriel and Justina their rights. But before appealing to the law he resolved upon submitting the whole case to Churchill Penwyn and to Justina, in order to discover the possibility of compromise. It would be a hard thing to reduce Churchill and his wife to beggary. They had spent their money wisely, and done good in the land. An equitable division of the estate would be better pleasing to Maurice's idea of justice than a strict exaction of legal rights, and he had little doubt that Justina would think with him.

His first duty was to go to her and tell her all the truth, and he lost no time in performing that duty. It was on Saturday morning that he found the letters in the loft, and on Saturday evening he was in London, with the quiet of Sunday before him in which to make his revelation.

He left a note for Justina at her lodgings,—

'DEAR MISS ELGOOD,

'Please do not go to church to-morrow morning, as I want to have a long talk with you on a serious business matter, and will call at eleven for that purpose.

'Yours always,

'MAURICE CLISSOLD.'

'SATURDAY EVENING.'

He found her ready to receive him next morning at eleven, fresh and fair in her simple autumn dress of fawn-coloured cashmere, with neat linen collar and cuffs, a blue ribbon and silver locket, her sole ornaments.

His letter had filled her with vague apprehensions which Matthew Elgood's arguments had not been able to dispel.

'What business can you have to talk about with me?' she asked, nervously, as she and Maurice shook hands. 'I hope it is nothing dreadful. Your letter has kept me in a fever ever since I received it.'

'I am sorry to hear that. I ought to have said less, or more. It is a serious business, but I hope not one that need give you pain, except so far as your tenderness and compassion may be concerned for others. The story I am going to tell you is a sad one, and has to do with your own infancy.'

'I can't understand,' she said, with a perplexed look.

'Don't try to understand until I have told you more. I shall make everything very clear to you in due time.'

'Papa may hear, I suppose?' said she, with a glance at the comedian, who had laid down his after-breakfast pipe, and was looking far from comfortable.

'Yes, I see no reason why Mr. Elgood should not hear all I have to say. He will be able to confirm some of my statements.'

Matthew Elgood moved uneasily in his chair, emptied the ashes from his pipe with a shaking hand, wiped his forehead with an enormous bandanna, and then burst out suddenly:

'Justina, Mr. Clissold is about to make a revelation. I know enough of its nature to know that it will be startling. I think I've done my duty by you, my girl; urged you on in your profession; taught you how to walk the stage, how to make a point; taught you Miss Farren's original business in Lady Teazle. We've shared and shared alike, through good and foul weather. Lear and his Fool couldn't have stuck better by each other. We've tramped the barren heath of life through storm and tempest, and if you've had to wear leaky shoes sometimes, why, so have I. And if you discover from Mr. Clissold,' pointing his pipe at Maurice with tremulous hand, 'that I am not so much your father as I might have been had nature intended me for that position, I hope your heart will speak for me, and confess that I have done a father's duty.'

With this closing appeal Mr. Elgood laid down his pipe, buried his face in the big bandanna, and sobbed aloud.

Justina was on her knees at his feet in a

moment, her arms around him, his grizzled head drawn down upon her shoulder, soothing, caressing him.

'Dear papa, what can you mean! Not my father?'

'No, my love,' sobbed the comedian. 'Legally, actually, as a matter of fact, I have no claim to that title. Morally, it is another pair of shoes. I held you at the baptismal font—I have fed you many a time when your sole refreshment was alike insipid and sloppy,—these hands have guided your infantine steps, yet, I am not your father. Legally I have no authority over you—or your salary.'

'You are my father all the same,' answered Justina, emphatically. 'What other father have I?'

'Your legal parent has certainly been conspicuous by his absence, my love. You were placed in my wife's arms on the day of your birth—an abandoned child—and from that hour to her death she honestly performed a mother's part.'

'And never had less than a mother's love!' cried Justina. 'Do not fear, dear papa, that anything I may hear to-day can ever lessen my affection for you. We have borne too much misfortune together not to love each other dearly,' she added, with a touch of sadness.

'Say on, sir!' exclaimed the actor, with an oratorical flourish of his bandanna; 'she is staunch, and I fear not the issue.'

Maurice told his story in plainest words—the story of Muriel's marriage and Muriel's sorrow. Justina heard him with tears of tenderness and pity.

'Now, Justina,' he said, after having explained everything, 'you understand that you have a legal claim to the Penwyn estate. Your grandfather's will bequeathed the property to George Penwyn, your father, or his issue, male or female. If a daughter inherited, her husband, whomsoever she married, was to assume the name of Penwyn. I have taken the trouble to read the will, and I have no doubt as to your position. You can file a bill in chancery—or your next friend for you—to-morrow, and you can oust Churchill Penwyn from house and land, wealth and social status. It will be rather hard upon his wife, who is a very sweet woman, and has done much good in her neighbourhood.'

'Do you think I want his money or his land?' cried Justina, indignantly. 'Not a sixpence—not a rood. I only want the name you say I have a right to bear—James Penwyn's name. To think that we were cousins! Poor James!'

'You dislike Churchill Penwyn. This would be a grand revenge for you.'

'I dislike him because I have never been able to rid myself of the idea that he had some hand, directly or indirectly, in his cousin's death. But I do not wish to injure him. I leave him to God and his own conscience. If he has sinned as I believe he has, life must be bitter to him—in spite of wealth and position.'

'Are you not intoxicated by the notion of being Lady of Penwyn Manor?' asked Maurice.

'No. I am content to be what I am—to earn my own bread, and live happily with poor old papa,' laying her hand lovingly on the comedian's shoulder.

A welcome hearing this for Maurice Clissold, who had feared lest change of fortune should work a fatal change in the girl he loved. But he suppressed all emotion, and went on in his business-like tone.

'Well, Justina, since you seem to regard your right to the Penwyn estate with supreme indifference, you will be the more likely to fall into my way of thinking. Looking at the case from an equitable standpoint, it does certainly appear to me that, although by the old Squire's will you are entitled to the whole of the property, it would be not the less an injustice were you to claim all. It would seem a hard thing to deprive Churchill Penwyn altogether of an estate which he has administered with judgment and benevolence. My idea, therefore, is that I, as your next friend, if you will allow me the privilege of that position, should state the case to Mr. Penwyn, and propose a compromise, namely, that he should mortgage the estate for a sum of money amounting to half its value, and should deliver that money to you. His income would in this manner be reduced by one-half, by the interest on this sum, and it would be at his discretion to save money, even with that smaller income, and lessen the amount of the mortgage out of his accumulations, as the years went on. I think this would be at once a fair and liberal proposal, making his change of fortune as light as possible.'

'I do not want any of his money,' said Justina, impetuously.

'My love, that is simply childish,' exclaimed Mr. Elgood.

'Let me act for you, Justina ; trust me to deal generously with the Squire and his wife.'

'I will trust you,' she answered, looking up at him with perfect faith and love.

'Trust me in this and in all things. You shall not find me unworthy of your confidence.'

And this was all that was said about the Penwyn estate. Maurice spent the rest of the day with Justina, took her to Westminster Abbey in the after- noon to hear a great preacher, and walked with her afterwards in the misty groves of St. James's Park, and then and there, feeling that he was now free to open his heart to her, told her in truest, tenderest words, how the happiness of his future life was bound up in her ; how, rich or poor, she was dearer to him than all the world beside.

And so, in the London fog and gloom, under the smoky metropolitan trees, they plighted their troth —Justina ineffably happy.

' I thought you did not care for me,' she said, when all had been told.

' I thought you only cared for James Penwyn's memory,' answered Maurice.

' Poor James!   That love was like a midsummer night's dream.'

' And this is reality ? '

' Yes.'

He held her to his beating heart under the autumnal trees, and kissed her with the kiss of betrothal.

' My love! my dearest! my truest! my best!— what is wealth or position, or all this bitter world can give and take away, measured against love like ours ? '   And after this homily, which Justina remembered a great deal better than the great preacher's sermon, they turned their faces homewards, and arrived just in time to prevent the utter ruin of the dinner, which their tardiness had imperilled.

VOL. III.   Q

' You wouldn't have liked to see a pretty little bit of beef like that reduced to the condition of a deal board, now, would you ?' asked Mr. Elgood, pointing to the miniature sirloin.

Maurice and Justina interchanged smiles. They were thinking that they would be content to dine upon deal boards henceforward, so long as they dined together.

CHAPTER XIII.

MAURICE CLISSOLD went back to Cornwall next day, with full powers, so far as Justina's interests were concerned. Her greatest anxiety was to see the unhappy mother from whom she had been severed since the hour of her birth ; but to bring about a meeting between these two was not the easiest thing in the world. Other interests were at stake. The Albert Theatre could not get on without Justina, or so the manager affirmed ; and Justina's engagement was for the entire season. No breaking it, save by forfeiture of reputation with the public, and at the hazard of a lawsuit.

The only thing to be done was to bring Muriel nearer London so soon as she should be strong enough to bear the journey. Maurice hoped much from the daughter's influence upon the mother's disordered brain. He was at Borcel End by eight o'clock in the evening—neither Mr. Trevanard nor his son suspecting that their erratic guest had been further than Seacomb—and found the aspect of things improving. Muriel was calmer; the burns had proved of the slightest, and all was going on favourably. He went in and sat by her bedside for a few minutes, and talked to her. The wan eyes looked at him calmly enough, but with a curious wonder. He found that she remembered nothing of the fire, and had no idea why she had been ill and in pain. But she did remember the promise he had made her about her daughter.

'Some one told me I should see my baby again,' she said. 'I don't know who it was, but some one told me so, and I know that I shall see her—when we meet our friends in heaven.'

'You shall see her here, on this earth,' said Maurice.

'Is that true?'

'Quite true.'

'Then let me go to sleep till she comes. Lay her here beside me, and let me find her here when I open my eyes—my sweet baby!'

' Consider how many years have come and gone since you saw her.   She is an infant no longer, but a beautiful young woman.'

Muriel stared at him with a puzzled look.   'I don't want to see any young women; I want my baby again—the little baby my mother stole from me.

This made things difficult.   Maurice saw in this a fond clinging to the past, memory strong enough to make the lapse of years as nothing.   He made no attempt to argue the point, but left Muriel to the devoted grandmother's care.

The blind woman sat in her easy chair by the bed, knitting industriously, and murmuring a soothing word now and then.   No voice had such power to comfort Muriel.

' When shall I see my niece, and when will you tell father ?' Martin asked, eagerly, directly he and Maurice were alone together.

' You shall see your niece as soon as your sister is strong enough to bear a journey, when you can bring her up to some quiet little place in the neighbourhood of London.   As for your father, I think my chain of evidence is now so complete that I

cannot tell him too soon. I will get a quiet hour
with him to-morrow after breakfast, if I can. Later
I am going to the Manor House to examine my
ground and discover if there is any chance of a
friendly compromise.

'I hope you'll be able to settle things pleasantly,'
said Martin. 'I can't bear the idea of those poor
young ladies—Mrs. Penwyn and Miss Bellingham—
being turned out of house and home.'

'It shall not be so bad as that, depend upon it,'
replied Maurice.

He was down early next morning, and asked
Mr. Trevanard for half an hour's conversation after
breakfast.

'An hour, if you like,' answered Michael, in his
listless way. 'There's not much for me to do upon
the farm. I only potter about; the men would get
on quite as well without me, I dare say.'

'I can't believe that, Mr. Trevanard,' said
Maurice, cheerily. 'The master's eye—you know
the old adage?'

'Bridget was the ruling mind, sir. Bridget was
worth twenty of me!'

It was a cold and blusterous morning—the dead leaves falling fast from the few trees about Borcel, but Michael and his companion were fond of the open air, so they went out into the neglected garden, a wilderness where Muriel had been wont to range alone and at liberty for the last twenty years.

Here, in a narrow path screened by hazel bushes, the farmer and Maurice Clissold paced up and down while Maurice told his story, taking care to soften Bridget Trevanard's part in the domestic tragedy, and to demonstrate that, when erring most, she had been actuated only by regard for the family honour, and a mistaken family pride.'

Michael heard him with deepest emotion.

'My poor girl!—my beautiful Muriel! You don't know how proud I was of her—how I doated on her and to think that I should never have suspected that all was not well, that my poor child was being ill-used in her own home.'

'Not ill-used,' remonstrated Maurice, pleading for the dead wife who had trusted him with her secret. 'There was no unkindness.'

'No unkindness? They made her suffer shame,

they refused to believe in her purity; was that no
unkindness? They robbed her of her child! For
what? The world's good word! I would have
stood between my darling and the world. None
should have dared to slander her while I was near.
What right had my wife to take this matter into
her own hands—to hoodwink me with her secrecies
and suppressions? I would have stood by my child.
Muriel would have trusted me. Yes, she would
have trusted her indulgent old father, even if she
feared to confide in her mother. Bridget was always
too severe.'

'Remember that your wife erred in her anxiety
for your good name.'

'Yes, yes, I know that. God knows, it goes hard
with me to speak against her in her grave—poor
faithful soul! She was faithful according to her
notion of right. But she took too much heed of
the world—her world—half a dozen families within
five miles of Borcel. The sun, and moon, and
heaven, and all God's angels were not so much
account to her. Poor soul! She must have suffered.
I've seen the lines of trouble growing deeper in her

face, and never knew why they came there. My poor, trampled-upon Muriel! It was a cruel thing to send away the child. I could have loved it dearly!'

'You will love her dearly still, when I bring her to you.'

'Yes, but not as I could have loved her twenty years ago—when she was a helpless infant. My firstborn grandchild.'

The idea that this grandchild of his was the rightful owner of the Penwyn estate, Borcel End included, moved Michael Trevanard but slightly. He was not calm enough to consider this business from a worldly point of view. He could only think of the grandchild that was born under his roof, and spirited away while he lay in his bed, unsuspecting of the evil that was being wrought for love of his good name. He could only think of the persecuted daughter whose life had been made so bitter—of the husband who had never lived to acknowledge his wife—the father who had never known of his child's birth. The thought of these things altogether absorbed his mind, and he scarcely realized the fact of his grandchild's claim to wealth and position.

'And where is she? What is she doing now—Muriel's daughter—my grandchild?' he asked.

Maurice explained Justina's position.

'What!' cried the old man, with a wry face, 'a play actress? Raddled red and white, and in short petticoats all over tinsel stars, capering outside a show?' his only notion of actresses was founded on his experiences at Seacomb cattle fair—'do you mean to say that my flesh and blood has come to that?'

Maurice hastened to correct the farmer's idea of the dramatic profession, and to assure him that his granddaughter was to all intents and purposes a lady; modest, refined in feeling and in manner, beautiful in mind and person, a grandchild of whom he had ample reason to be proud.

'A London theatre is not in the least like those itinerant playhouses you have seen at Seacomb fair,' he said.

'Humph! They don't dance outside, I suppose? or play the Pandean pipes, and beat a gong?'

'Nothing approaching it.   You might mistake a London theatre for a church, looking at its outside.'

' And they don't raddle their faces, eh ?'

'Oh dear no! Maurice replied, with a faint twinge in that region of his sensorium which phrenologists appropriate to conscientiousness. 'Not in the least.   In short, acting in London is high art.'

' And no short petticoats and tinsel stars, eh ?'

' No tinsel stars!   Nor does your granddaughter ever appear in short petticoats.   She is a most re-fined and elegant actress, and I know that whether you see her on or off the stage, you will be equally charmed with her.'

'I shall love her for Muriel's sake,' answered Michael Trevanard, tenderly.   'Yes, I should love her dearly ; even if she raddled her cheeks and danced outside a show at a fair !'

CHAPTER XIV.

Two hours later Maurice Clissold was at the gate
of Penwyn Manor. The girl Elspeth admitted him.
she had bound up her coarse black hair, which had
been rough and wild as a mustang's mane when he
last saw her, and wore a neat stuff gown and a clean
white muslin cap, instead of the picturesque half
gipsy costume she had worn on that former occasion.
This at least was a concession to Mrs. Penwyn's
tastes, and argued that even Elspeth's impish nature
had been at last brought under Madge's softening
influence.

'Anything amiss with your grandmother?' asked
Maurice, surprised at not seeing that specimen of
the Meg Merrilies tribe.

'Yes, sir, she's very ill.'

'What is the matter with her?'

'Bilious fever,' answered the girl, curtly; and Maurice passed on. He had no leisure now to concern himself about Rebecca Mason, though he had in no wise forgotten those curious facts which made her presence at Penwyn Manor a mystery.

There were more dead leaves drifting about than on his last visit, and the advance of Autumn had made itself obvious in decay, which all the industry of gardeners could not conceal. The pine groves were strewn with fallen cones. The chestnuts were dropping their prickly green balls, the chrysanthemums and China asters had a ragged look, the glory of the geranium tribe was over, and even those combinations of colour which modern gardeners contrive from flowerless plants seemed to lose all glow and brightness under the dull grey sky. To Maurice's mind, knowing that he was a messenger of trouble, the Manor House had a gloomy look.

He asked to see the Squire, and was ushered at once into the library, a room which Churchill had built. It was lighted from the top by a large ground-glass dome, and was lined from floor to ceiling with bookcases of ebonized wood, relieved with narrow lines of gold. In each of the four angles stood a pedestal of dark green serpentine, surmounted by a marble bust—Dante, Shakespeare, Voltaire, Goethe, the four great representatives of European literature. A noble room, filled with the noblest books. Such a room as a man, having made for himself, would love as if it were a sentient thing. These books, looking down upon him on every side, were as the souls of the mighty dead. Here, shut in from the outer world, he could never be companionless.

Churchill was seated at a table reading. He started up at Maurice's entrance, and received him courteously, cordially even, so far as words may express cordiality, but with a sudden troubled look which did not escape Maurice, transient as it was.

'Glad to see you here again, Clissold; but why didn't you go straight to the ladies? You'll find them in the hall. Most of our friends have left us, so you'll be quite an acquisition this dull weather.'

'You are very good, but I regret to say that the business which brings me here to-day denies me the right to approach Mrs. Penwyn. I come as a harbinger of trouble.'

Churchill's face whitened to the lips, and his thin nervous hand fastened with a tight grip upon the edge of the table against which he stood, as if he could scarcely have held himself erect without that support.

'How frightened he looks!' thought Maurice. 'A man of his type oughtn't to be wanting in moral courage.'

'And pray what is the nature of your evil tidings?' Churchill asked, recovering self-control His resolute nature speedily asserted itself. A faint tinge of colour came back to his sunken cheeks; his eyes lost their look of sudden horror, and assumed a hard, defiant expression.

'This property—the Penwyn estate—is very dear to you, I think?' interrogated Maurice.

'It is as dear to me as a man's birthright should naturally be to him; and it has been the happy home of my married life.' This with a touch of tenderness. In no moment of his existence, however troubled, could he speak of Madge without tenderness.

'Yet Penwyn can be hardly called your birthright, since you inherit it by an accident,' said

Maurice, nervously, anxious to take the edge off his unpleasant communication.

'What is the drift of these remarks, Mr. Clissold? They seem to me entirely purposeless, and pardon me if I add, somewhat impertinent.'

'Mr. Penwyn, I am here to inform you that there is a member of your family in existence who possesses a prior claim to this estate.'

'You are dreaming, sir, or you are deceived by some impostor. I and my child are the sole representatives of the Penwyn family.'

'There are secrets in every family, Mr. Penwyn. There has been a secret in your family, religiously kept for more than twenty years, but lately brought to light; in some part by my agency.'

'What, sir, you have come into this house as a spy, while you have been secretly assailing my position as inheritor of my cousin's estate?'

'I have not entered your house since I made the discovery I speak of.'

'Your discovery has come about with marvellous rapidity, then, for it is not long since you were my guest.'

'My discovery has been arrived at **quickly**.'

'**Pray** acquaint me **with the** nature **of** this mare's-nest.'

'I have to inform you that your **uncle,** George Penwyn, before leaving England for **the** last time, privately married the daughter of his father's tenant, Michael **Trevanard, of** Borcel End.'

Churchill Penwyn laughed contemptuously.

'I congratulate you upon having hit upon about **the most improbable story I ever heard of!'** he said. '**My** uncle, George **Penwyn,** married **to** old Trevanard's daughter! and nobody upon earth aware of the fact till you, a stranger, unearthed it? A likely story, Mr. Clissold!'

'**Likely** or unlikely, it is true, and I have sufficient evidence **to** prove **it, or** I should not have broached the subject to you. I have in my possession a certified copy of the entry in the marriage register at **St. John's** Church, Didmouth, Devonshire; **and** five **letters in** your uncle's hand, acknowledging Muriel Trevanard as his wife; also a sealed letter from the same, committing her to the **care of the** late Mr. Tomlin, solicitor, of Seacomb, in the event of her needing that gentleman's protection during her husband's absence. Nor do I rely upon documentary evidence alone. The vicar of Didmouth, who married your uncle to Miss Trevanard, is still alive; and the principal witness of the marriage, Muriel's friend and confidante, is ready to support the claim of Muriel's daughter should you force her to appeal to the law, instead of seeing, as I hope you will see, the advisability of an equitable compromise. Miss Penwyn has no desire to exact her legal rights. She has empowered me to suggest a fair and honourable alternative.'

Maurice proceeded to give a brief outline of Justina's case, and to suggest his own idea of an equitable settlement.

Churchill sat with folded arms, and gloomy face bent downward listening. This story of Maurice Clissold's seemed to him, so far, hardly worth serious thought. It was so wildly improbable, so like the dream of a fevered brain, that any claimant should come forward to dispute his hold of wealth and station. Yet he told himself that Clissold was no fool, and would hardly talk of documentary evidence which he was unprepared to produce. On the other hand, this Clissold might be a villain, and the whole business a conspiracy.

'Let me see your copy of the register, sir,' Churchill said, authoritatively.

Maurice took a paper from his breast-pocket, and laid it on Mr. Penwyn's desk. Yes. It was formal enough.

'George Penwyn, bachelor, gentleman, of Penwyn Manor, to Muriel Trevanard, spinster, daughter of Michael Trevanard, farmer, of Borcel End. The witnesses, Maria Barlow, spinster, schoolmistress, of Seacomb ; and James Pope, clerk, Didmouth.' If this were a genuine copy of an existing entry there would be no doubt as to the fact of George Penwyn's marriage.

Both gentlemen were too much engrossed at this moment—Churchill pondering the significance of the document in his hand, Maurice watching his countenance as he meditated—to be aware of the opening of a door near the fireplace, a door which fitted into the bookcase, and was masked with

dummy books. This door was gently opened, a
woman's face looked in for an instant, and was
quickly withdrawn.   But the door, although apparently closed, was not shut again.

'And you pretend that there was issue to this
marriage ? ' said Churchill.

'The lady whose claim I am here to assert is
the daughter of Mr. George Penwyn, by that
marriage.'

'And pray where has this young lady been
hiding herself all her 'life, and how is it that she
has suffered her rights to be in abeyance all this
time ? '

'She was brought up in ignorance of her
parentage.'

'Oh ! I understand,' cried Churchill, scornfully.
'Some Miss Jones, or Smith, who has taken it into
her wise young head—inspired doubtless by some
astute friend—that she may as well prove herself a
Penwyn, if she can. And you come to me with this
liberal offer of a compromise to take half my estate
in the most off-hand way. Upon my word, Mr
Clissold, you and this scheme of yours are a little

too absurd. I can't even allow myself to be angry with you. That would be taking the thing too seriously.'

'Remember, Mr. Penwyn, if I leave this house without arriving at some kind of understanding with you I shall place the matter in the hands of my solicitors without delay, and the law must take its course. However protracted or costly the process by which Miss Penwyn may obtain her rights, I have no doubt as to the ultimate issue. She would have been contented with half your fortune. The law, if it give her anything will give her all.'

'So be it. I will fight her to the bitter end. First and foremost, this marriage, supposing this document to be genuine,' bringing down his clenched fist upon the paper, and with an evil upward look at Maurice, 'is no marriage!'

'What do you mean?"

'A marriage with a person of unsound mind is no marriage. It is void in law. There is Blackstone to refer to if you doubt me,' pointing to a set of volumes in dark brown Russia. 'Now, Muriel, the daughter of Michael Trevanard, has been deranged for the last twenty years. It is a notorious fact to everybody in the neighbourhood.'

'When that marriage took place, and for a year after the marriage, Muriel was as sane as you or I. Her brain was turned by the shock she experienced upon being informed suddenly of her husband's awful death. I can bring forward sufficient witnesses to prove the state of her mind up to that time. And again you are to remember that the same authority you have just quoted tells you that no marriage is voidable after the death of either of the contracting parties.'

'And you are prepared to prove that this young woman—this waif and stray, brought up without the knowledge of her name or parentage—is the legitimate daughter of my uncle, George Penwyn, and Muriel, his wife. Go your ways, Mr. Clissold, and make the best use of your evidence, documentary or otherwise. I will stand by my rights against you, and would stand by them against a stronger cause than yours.'

He touched a spring bell, which stood on his desk, —a summons answered with extreme promptitude.

'The door,' said the Squire, resuming his book, without so much as a parting glance at his visitor.

Maurice was conducted to the porch, and left the house without having seen Mrs. Penwyn or her sister. He was bitterly disappointed by the result of his morning's work, which had proved compromise impossible, and left no course open to him save the letter of the law.

*　.*　　*　　*　　*

Scarcely had the library door closed on Maurice Clissold, when the other door, which had been left ajar during the latter part of the interview, was quietly opened, and Madge Penwyn stole to her husband's side, knelt down by him, and wound her arms round his neck. He had been sitting with his face buried in his hands, trying to think out his position, when he found her arms about him, his head drawn gently against her shoulder.

'Dearest! I have heard all,' she said, quietly.

'You heard! Madge?" he exclaimed, with a startled look. 'Well, my love, it matters very little. It is all the merest folly. There is no possibility of what this man threatens.'

'Churchill — husband—my beloved,' she began with deepest feeling. 'You do not mean to oppose this claim ?'

'To the death.'

'What? Surely you will accept the truth—if it is the truth—and surrender fortune and estate. Oh' welcome change of fortune, love, that brings some measure of atonement. I have never told you how hateful, how horrible all our wealth and luxury has been to me since I have known——"

'Hush, Madge ! You know so much that you should know enough to be wise. Do you think I am going to surrender these things ? Do you think I am the kind of man to sit down tamely and let a rogue hatch a conspiracy to rob me of wealth and status ? They have cost me too dear.'

'They have cost you so dear that you can never have joy or peace with them, Churchill. God shows us this way of getting rid of our burden. If you have any hope of mercy, any desire to be forgiven, resign this fortune. It is the price of iniquity. You can know no true repentance while you retain it. If I had seen any way of your surrendering this estate before now without exciting suspicion of the dreadful truth, I should have urged the sacrifice upon you. I urge it now, with all the strength of my love.'

'It is useless, Madge. I could not go back to poverty, laborious days and nights, the struggle for daily bread. I could not lead that kind of life again.'

'Not with me, Churchill? We could go away, to the other end of the world. To Australia, where life is simpler and easier than in England. We could know peace again; for you might dare to hope, if your sacrifice were freely made, that God had accepted it as an atonement.'

'Can I atone to the dead? Will James Penwyn, in his untimely grave, be any better off because some impostor riots in the wealth that ought to have been his? A left-handed atonement that!'

'But if you find that this girl is no impostor?'

'The lawyers will have to decide that. If she can establish her right, you and I, and our boy, will have to say good-bye to Penwyn.'

' Happy loss if it lighten the burden of your sin.
Do you think that I shall be sorry to leave this
place, Churchill ? I have never known peace here
since——'

She threw herself upon his breast with a shud-
dering sigh.

' Madge, my dearest, my angel of love and compassion, be content to abide the issue of events.
Leave all to me.'

' No, Churchill,' she answered, raising her head,
and looking at him with grave and earnest eyes, ' I
am not content. You know that since that bitter
day I have left you in peace. I have not wearied
you with my tears. I have suffered in secret, and
have made it the chief duty of my life to lighten
your burden, so far as in me lay. But I can be
content no longer. The wealth that has weighed
upon my soul can now be given up, with honour.
The world can find no subject for slander in your
quiet surrender of an estate for which a new
claimant has arisen. And we can begin life afresh
together, love, your soul purified by sacrifice, your
conscience lightened, your peace made with God.

We can begin life anew in some distant land, humbly, toilfully ; so far away from all past cares, that your wrong-doing may seem no more than the memory of an evil dream, and all the future open for manifold good deeds that shall weigh against that one dreadful sin.'

She seemed like an angel pleading with him for the salvation of his soul, yet he resisted her.

' It is useless, Madge. You do not know what you are talking about. I could not live a life of obscurity. It would be moral suicide.'

' Will you choose between me and fortune, Churchill ? '

' What do you mean ? '

' That unless you give up this estate you must give up me. I will live here no longer, share your ill-gotten wealth no longer !'

' Think of your boy.'

' I do think of him. God forbid that my son should ever inherit Penwyn. There is the curse of blood upon every rood of land. Let it pass into other hands—guiltless hands !'

' Give me time to think, Madge ; you bewilder me by this sudden attack.'

'Think as long as you like, dearest; only decide rightly at last.' And with one long kiss upon his pale forehead, she left him.

Once alone, he set himself to think out his position—to face this new aspect of things.

Could this alleged heiress—impostor or not—rob him of his estate? Was it possible for George Penwyn's marriage, and the identity of George Penwyn's child, to be proved in a court of law; proved so indisputably as to dislodge him from his position as possessor of the estate?

'No,' he told himself, 'the strength will be all on my side. The law does not encourage claimants of this stamp. If it did, no man's estate would be secure, no real property would be worth ten years purchase.'

He had taken a high tone with Maurice Clissold ; had affected to regard the whole matter as an absurdity, but now, face to face with the facts that had been put before him, he felt that the question was serious, and that he could not be too prompt in action.

He looked at a railway time-table, and found

that he would have just time enough to catch the next up train from Seacomb, a slowish train, not reaching London till late in the evening.

'I will go up to town and see Pergament,' he said to himself, as he touched the bell.

'Tell them to bring round the dog-cart at once. I shall want Hunter.'

'Any particular horse, sir?'

'Yes, Wallace.'

Wallace was the fastest horse in the stable—always excepting the Squire's favourite, Tarpan, which had never been degraded by harness.

While the dog-cart was being got ready, Churchill wrote to his wife,

'MY DEAREST,

'I am going to London to inquire into this business. Be calm, be brave, as befits my noble wife.

'Your own till death,

'C. P.'

This brief note addressed and sealed, the Squire went upstairs to his dressing-room, crammed a few things into his travelling bag, and went down to the porch with the bag in his hand, just as the dog-cart drove up. Wallace, a big, deep-chested bay, in admirable condition, fresh and eager for the start; the groom breathless, having dressed himself against time.

Churchill took the reins, and the light vehicle was soon spinning along that well-made road with which the Squire of Penwyn had improved his property. Less than an hour, and Mr. Penwyn was seated in a railway carriage on his way to London.

He was at Mr. Pergament's office early next morning; indeed, more than half an hour before the arrival of that gentleman, who came in at ten o'clock, fresh and sleek of aspect, with a late tea-rosebud in the buttonhole of his glossy blue coat.

Great was the solicitor's astonishment at beholding Churchill.

'My dear Mr. Penwyn, this *is* a surprise. One does not expect to see a man of your standing in town in the dead season. Indeed, even I, a humble working bee in the great hive, have been thinking of getting as far as Aix-les-Bains, or Spa. But you are not looking well. You look careworn—fagged.'

‘ I have reason to look so,’ answered Churchill : and then explained the motive of his journey.

He told Mr. Pergament all that Clissold had told him, without reserve, with a wonderful precision and clearness. The lawyer listened intently, and with gravest concern.

But before he said a word in reply, Mr. Pergament unlocked a tin case inscribed ‘ Penwyn,’ took out a document, and read it from the first line to the last.

‘ What is that ? ’ asked Churchill.

‘ A copy of your grandfather’s will. I want to be quite sure how you stand as regards this claimant.’

‘ Well ? ’

‘ I am sorry to say that the will is dead against you. If this person can be proved to be the daughter of George Penwyn, she would take the estate, under your grandfather’s will. There is no doubt of that.’

‘ But how is she to prove her identity with the child said to be born at Borcel End, and whose birth was made such a secret ? ’

'Difficult, perhaps; but if she has been in the charge of the same people all her life, and those people are credible witnesses——'

'Credible witnesses!' cried Churchill, contemptuously. 'The man who has brought up this girl belongs to the dregs of society, and if, by a little hard swearing he can foist this stray adoption of his upon society as the rightful owner of the Penwyn estate, do you suppose he will shrink from a little more or less perjury? Credible witnesses! No man's property in the land is secure if claimants such as this can arise "to push us from our stools." '

'This Mr. Clissold is a gentleman, and a man of good family, is he not?'

'He belongs to decent people, I believe, but that is no reason why he should not be an adventurer. There are plenty of well-born adventurers in the world.'

'No doubt, no doubt,' replied Mr. Pergament, blandly. In his private capacity, as a Christian and a gentleman, he was benevolently sympathetic; but the idea of a contested estate was not altogether unpleasing to his professional mind.

' Who are Mr. Clissold's lawyers ? '

' Messrs. Willgross and Harding."

' A highly respectable firm—old established—in every way reputable. I do not think they would take up a speculative case.'

' I do not feel sure that they will take up this case, though Mr. Clissold appeared to think so,' answered Churchill. ' However, your business is to be prepared. Remember, I shall fight this to the bitter end. Let them prove the marriage if they can. It will be for our side to deny that there was ever any issue of that marriage.'

' Humph,' mused the lawyer. ' There, assuredly, lies the weakness of their case. Child's birth not registered, child brought up by strolling player. Yes, we will fight, Mr. Penwyn. Pray keep your mind easy. I will get counsel's opinion without delay if you desire it, and I suppose in a case so nearly affecting your interests you would prefer an unprejudiced opinion to being your own adviser. The best men shall be secured for our side.'

' Which do you call the best men ? '

Mr. Pergament named three of the most illustrious lights of the equity bar.

'Very good men in their way, no doubt,' said Churchill, 'but I would rather have Shinebarr, Shandrish, and—say, McStinger.'

Mr. Pergament looked horrified.

'My dear sir, clever men, but unscrupulous, notoriously unscrupulous.'

'My dear Pergament, when a gang of swindlers hatch a conspiracy to deprive me of house and home, I don't want my rights defended by scrupulous men.'

'But, really, Shandrish, a man I never gave a brief to in my life,' remonstrated the solicitor.

'What does that signify? It is my battle we have to fight, and you must let me choose my weapons.'

CHAPTER XV.

HAVING seen the chief representative of Pergament
and Pergament, placed his interests in the hands of
that respectable house, and chosen the advocates
who were to defend his cause, should this pretended
cousin of his dare to assert her rights in a court of
law, Churchill Penwyn felt himself free to go back
to Cornwall by the mid-day train. He had an uneasy
feeling in being away from home at this juncture—
a vague sense of impending peril on all sides—a
passionate desire to be near his wife and child.

He had ample time for thought during that long
journey westward; time to contemplate his position
in all its bearings, to wonder whether his wisdom
might not, after all, be folly, beside Madge's clear-
sighted sense of right.

'She spoke the bitter truth,' he thought. 'Wealth

and estate have not brought me happiness. They
have gratified my self-esteem, satisfied my ambition,
but they have not given me restful nights or peaceful dreams. Would it be better for me to please
Madge, throw up the sponge, and go to the other
end of the world, to begin life afresh, remote from
all old associations, out of reach of the memory of
the past?'

'No!' he told himself, after a pause. 'There
is no new life for me. I am too old for beginning
again.'

He thought of his triumphs of last session, those
bursts of fervid eloquence which had startled the
House into the admission that a new orator had
arisen, as when the younger Pitt first demonstrated
to the doubtful senate that he was a worthy son of
the great Commoner.

He was just at the beginning of a brilliant Parliamentary career, and with him ambition was an
all-powerful passion. To let these things go, even
for Madge's sake, would be too great a sacrifice.
And his boy, was he to bequeath nothing to that
beloved son? Neither fortune nor name?'

' I could more easily surrender Penwyn than my chances of personal distinction,' he said to himself.

It was nine o'clock in the evening when he arrived at Seacomb. He had telegraphed for his groom to meet him with the dog-cart; and, as the train steamed slowly into the station, he saw the lamps of that well-appointed vehicle shining across the low rail which divided the platform from the road. A dark night for a drive by that wild moorland way.

'Shall I drive, sir?' asked the groom.

'No,' Churchill answered shortly; and the next minute they were flying through the darkness. The light vehicle swayed from side to side on the stony road.

'It would be a short cut out of all my difficulties if I were to come to grief somewhere between this and the Manor House,' thought Churchill. 'A sudden fall upon a heap of stones, a splintered skull, an inquest, and all over. Poor Madge! It would be bad for her, but a relief perhaps—who can tell? She has owned that her life has been bitterness since that fatal day! Her very love for me is a kind of martyrdom. Poor Madge! If it was not a cowardly thing to give up all at the first alarm, I very believe I could bring myself to turn my back upon Penwyn Manor, take my wife and child out to Sydney, and try my luck as a barrister in a colonial court. For her sake —for her sake! Would not the humblest life be happiness with her?'

Things seemed to take a new shape to him during that swift homeward drive. He passed the shadowy plantations — the trees of his planting—bowled smoothly along the well-made road that crossed his own estate, and thought with a curious wonder, how little actual happiness his possessions had given him —how small a matter it would be, after all, to lose them.

The lighted windows of the north lodge shone out upon him as he mounted the crest of the last hill, and saw Manor House and gardens, pine groves and shrubberies, before him.

'Rebecca is keeping later hours than usual, isn't she?' he asked.

'She's very ill, sir, at death's door, they do say,' answered the groom, " but that queer young grand-daughter of hers has kept it dark, as long as she could, on account of the drink being at the bottom of it, begging your pardon sir.'

'Do you mean that Rebecca drinks ? '

' Well, yes, sir, on the quiet ; I believe she have always been inclined that way. Excuse me for mentioning it, sir, but you see a master is always the last to hear of these things.'

They were at the gates by this time. Elspeth came out of the lodge as they drove up.

' Take the dog-cart round to the stables, Hunter,' said Churchill, alighting. 'I am going in to see Rebecca.'

'Oh, sir, your dear lady is here—with grand-mother,' said Elspeth.

' My wife ? '

' Yes, sir. She came down this afternoon, hearing grandmother was so bad. And Mrs. Penwyn wouldn't have any one else to nurse her, though she's been raving and going on awful.'

Churchill answered not a word, but snatched the

candle from the girl's hand, and went up the narrow staircase. A wild, hoarse scream told him where the sick woman was lying. He opened the door, and there, in a close room, whose fever-tainted atmosphere seemed stifling and poisonous after the fresh night air, he saw his wife kneeling by a narrow iron bedstead, holding the gipsy's bony frame in her arms. He flung open the casement as wide as it would go. The cold night breeze rushed into the little room, almost extinguishing the candle.

'Madge! are you mad? Do you know the danger of being in this fever-poisoned room?'

'I know that there would have been danger for you had I not been here, Churchill,' his wife answered gently. 'I have been able to keep others out, which nothing less than my influence would have done. Half the gossips of Penwyn village would have been round this wretched creature's bed but for me. And her ravings have been dreadful,' with a shudder.

'What has she talked about?'

'All that happened—at Eborsham—that night,' answered Madge, in an awe-stricken whisper. 'She has forgotten no detail. Again and again, again and again, she has repeated the same words. But Mr. Price says she cannot last many hours—life is ebbing fast.'

'Did Price hear her raving?'

'Not much. She was quieter while he was here, and I was trying to engage his attention, to prevent his taking much notice of her wild talk.'

'Oh, Madge, Madge, what have you not borne for me! And now you expose yourself to the risk of typhoid fever for my sake.'

'There is no risk of typhoid. This poor creature is dying of delirium-tremens, Mr. Price assured me. She has lived on brandy for ever so long, and brain and body are alike exhausted.'

A wild scream broke from Rebecca's pale lips, and then, with an awful distinctness, Churchill heard her tell the story of his crime.

'Drunk was I?' cried the gipsy, with a wild laugh. 'Not so drunk but I could see—not so drunk but I could hear. I heard him fire the shot. I saw him creep out from behind the hedge. I saw him wipe his blood-stained hands. I have the handker-

chief still. It's worth more to me than a love-token
—-it's helped me to a comfortable home. Brandy—
give me some brandy, my throat is like a lime-
kiln!'

Madge took a glass of weak brandy and water
from the table, and held it to the tremulous lips.
The gipsy drank eagerly, but frowningly, and then
struggled to free herself from Madge Penwyn's em-
brace.

'Let me get at the bottle,' she gasped. 'I don't
want the cat-lap you give me!'

'Let me hold her,' said Churchill. 'Go home,
dearest, I will stop to the end.'

'No, Churchill, you would be less patient than I.
And if you nursed her it would set people talking,
while it is only natural for me to be with her.'

Elspeth opened the door a little way and peeped
in, asking if she could be useful.

'No, Elspeth, there is nothing for you to do. I
have done all Mr. Price directed. Go to bed, child,
and sleep if you can. There is nothing more to be
done.'

'And she'll die before the night is out, perhaps,'

said the girl, with a horror-stricken look at the emaciated figure on the bed. 'Mr. Price told me there was no hope.'

'You should not have let her drink so much, Elspeth,' said Madge gently.

'How could I help it ?   If I'd refused to fetch her the brandy she would have turned me out of doors, and I should have had to go on the tramp ; and that would have been hard after I'd got used to sleeping in a house, and having my victuals regular.   I daren't refuse to do anything she asked me for fear of the strap.   She wouldn't hesitate about laying in to me.'

'Poor, unhappy child.   There, go to your room and lie down.   I will take care of you henceforward, Elspeth.'

The girl said not a word, but came gently in to the room, knelt down by Mrs. Penwyn, and took up the hem of her dress and kissed it, an almost Oriental expression of gratitude and submission.

'I've heard tell about angels, but I never believed in 'em till I came to know you,' she said tearfully, and then left the room.

Rebecca had sunk back upon the pillow exhausted. Madge sat beside her, prepared for the next interval of delirium. Churchill stood by the window, looking out at the pine grove, and the dark sea beyond.

And thus the night wore on, and at daybreak, just when the slate-coloured sea looked coldest, and the east wind blew sharp and chill, and the shrill cry of chanticleer rang loud from the distant farmyard, Rebecca Mason's troubled spirit passed to the land of rest, and Churchill Penwyn knew that the one voice which could denounce him was silenced for ever.

Before breath |had departed from that wasted frame the Squire had examined all boxes and drawers in the room—they were not many—lest any record of his secret should lurk among the gipsy's few possessions. He had gone downstairs to the sitting-room for the same purpose, and had found nothing. Afterwards, when all was over, he found a little bundle rolled up in a tattered old bird's-eye neckerchief under the dead woman's pillow. It contained a few odd coins, and the handkerchief with which James Penwyn's murderer had wiped his ensanguined hand. All Churchill's influence had been too little to extort this hideous memento from the gipsy while life remained to her. Madge was kneeling by the open window, her face hidden, absorbed in silent prayer, when her husband discovered this hoarded treasure. He took it down to the room below, thrust it among the smouldering ashes of the wood fire, and watched it burn to a grey scrap of tinder which fluttered away from the hearth.

A little after daybreak, Elspeth was up and dressed, and had sped off to the village in search of a friendly gossip, who was wont to perform the last offices for poor humanity. To this woman Madge resigned her charge.

'Lord bless you, ma'am!' cried the village dame, lost in admiration. 'To think that a sweet young creature like you should leave your beautiful home to nurse a poor old woman!'

Madge and her husband went home in the cold autumn dawn—grave and silent both—with faces that looked wan and worn in the clear grey light.

Some of the household had sat up all night. Churchill's body servant, Mrs. Penwyn's maid, and an underling to wait upon those important personages.

'There is a fire in your dressing-room, ma'am,' said Mills, the maid. 'Shall I get you tea or coffee?'

'You can bring me some tea presently.' And to the dressing-room Mr. and Mrs. Penwyn went.

'Madge,' said Churchill, when Mills had brought the tea-tray, and been told she would be rung for when her services were required, and husband and wife were alone together,—'if I had needed to be assured of your devotion, to-night would have proved it to me. But I had no need of such assurance, and to-night is but one more act of self-sacrificing love—one more bond between us. It shall be as you wish, dearest. I will resign fortune and status, and lead the life you bid me lead. If I sinned for your sake—and I at least believed that I so sinned, —I will repent for your sake, and whatever atone-ment there may be in the sacrifice of this estate, it shall be made.

'Churchill, my own true husband.'

She was on her knees by his side, her head

lying against his breast, her eyes looking up at him with love unspeakable.

'Will this sacrifice set your heart at rest, Madge?'

'It will, dear love, for I believe that Heaven will accept your atonement.'

'Remember, it is in my option, however strong these people's case may be, to compromise matters, to retain the estate, and only surrender half the income—to hold my place in the county—to be to all effects and purposes Squire of Penwyn, to have the estate and something over three thousand a year to live upon. That course is open to us. These people will take half our fortune and be content. If I surrender what they are willing to leave me it is tantamount to throwing three thousand a year into the gutter. Shall I do that, Madge?'

'If you wish me to know rest or peace, love. I can know neither while we retain one sixpence of James Penwyn's money.'

'It shall be done then, my dearest. But remember that in making this sacrifice you perhaps doom your son to a life of poverty. And poverty is bitter, Madge. We have both felt its sting.'

'Providence will take care of my son.'

'So be it, Madge. You have chosen.'

She put her arms round his neck and kissed him.

'My dearest, now I am sure that you love me,' she said, gently.

'Madge, you are shivering. The morning air has chilled you,' exclaimed her husband, anxiously. And then turning her face towards him, he looked at her long and earnestly.

The vivid morning light, clear and cold, showed him every line in that expressive face. He scrutinized it with sharpest pain. Never till this moment had he been fully aware of the change which secret anguish had wrought in his wife's beauty, the gradual decay which had been going on before his eyes, unobserved in the pre-occupation of his mind.'

'My love, how ill you are looking!' he said, anxiously.

'I am not ill, Churchill. I have been unhappy, but that is all past now. That woman's presence at our gates was a perpetual horror to me. She is gone, and I seem to breathe more freely. This sacrifice of yours will bring peace to us both. I feel assured of that. In a new world, among new faces, we shall forget, and God will be good to us. He will forgive——' A burst of hysterical sobs interrupted her words, and for once in her life Madge Penwyn lost all power of self-control. Her weakness did not last long. Before Churchill could summon Mills his wife had recovered herself, and smiled at him, even with a pale wan smile.

'I am a little tired, dear, that is all. I will go to bed for an hour or two.'

'Rest as long as you can, dear. I will write to Pergament while you are sleeping, and ask him to make immediate arrangements for our voyage to Sydney. That Mills seems a faithful girl,' speaking of his wife's maid, 'she might go with us, as Nugent's nurse.

'No, dear. I shall take no nurse. I am quite able to wait upon my pet. We must begin life in a very humble way, and I am not going to burden you with a servant.'

'It shall be as you please, dear. Perhaps, after

all, I may not do so badly in the new country. I shall take my parliamentary reputation as a recommendation.'

Madge left him. She looked white and weak as some pale flower that had been beaten down by wind and rain. Churchill went to his dressing-room, refreshed his energies with a shower bath, dressed in his usual careful style, and went down to the dining-room at the sound of the breakfast-bell. Viola was there when he entered, playing with Nugent, which small personage was the un-failing resource of the ladies of the household in all intervals of *ennui*.

The little fellow screamed with delight at sight of his father. Churchill took him in his arms, and kissed him fondly, while Viola rang for the nurse.

'Good morning, Churchill. I did not know you had come back. What a rapid piece of business your London expedition must have been!'

'Yes, I did not care about wasting much time. What were you doing yesterday, Viola?'

'I spent the day with the Vyvyans, at the

Hall.   **They had a** wind-up croquet match.   It was great fun.'

'And you were not home till late, I suppose ?'

'Not so very late.   It was only half-past nine o'clock, but Madge had retired.   What **makes her so late this morning ?'**

Viola evidently knew nothing of her sister's visit to the lodge.

'She was engaged in a **work** of charity last night, and is worn out with fatigue.'

He told Viola how Madge had **nursed the dying** woman.

'That woman she disliked so much!   Was there ever such a noble heart as my sister's ?' cried Viola.

The form of breakfast gone through, and appear**ances thus maintained,** Churchill went up to his dressing-room, **where he had a** neat, business-like **oak** Davenport, and a small iron safe let into the wall, in **which he** kept his **bankers' book** and all important papers.

He had been spending very nearly **up to his** income during his reign at Penwyn.   **His improve**ments had absorbed a **good** deal of money, and he had spared nothing that would embellish or substantially improve the estate. The half-year's rents had not long been got in, however, and he had a balance of over two thousand pounds at his bankers. This, which he could draw out at once, would make a decent beginning for his new life. His wife's jewels were worth at least two thousand more, exclusive of those gems which he had inherited under the old Squire's will, and which would naturally be transferred with the estate. It was a hard thing for Churchill to write to Mr. Pergament, formally surrendering the estate, and leaving it to the lawyer to investigate the claim of Justina Penwyn, *alias* Elgood, and—if that claim were a just one—to effect the transfer of the property to that lady, without any litigation whatsoever.

'Pergament will think me mad,' he said to himself, as he signed this letter. 'However, I have kept my promise to Madge. My poor girl! I did not know till I looked in her face this morning what hard lines care had written there.'

He wrote a second letter to his bankers, directing them to invest sixteen hundred in Grand Trunk of

Canada First Preference Bonds, a security of which the interest was not always immediately to be relied upon, but which could be realized without trouble at any moment. He told them also to send him four hundred pounds in notes—tens, twenties, fifties.

His third letter was to the agents of a famous Australian line, telling them to reserve a state cabin for himself and wife, in the *Merlin*, which was to sail in a week, and enclosing a cheque for fifty pounds on account of the passage money.

'I have left no time for repentance, or change of plans,' he said to himself.

His letters despatched by the messenger who was wont to carry the postbag to Penwyn village, Churchill went to his wife's room. The blinds were closely drawn, shutting out the sunlight. Madge was sleeping soundly, but heavily—and the anxious husband fancied that her breathing was more laboured than usual. Her cheek, so pale when he had seen her last, was now flushed to a vivid crimson, and the hand he gently touched as he bent over her was dry and burning.

He went downstairs and out to the stables,

where he told Hunter, the groom, to put Wallace in the dog-cart and drive over to Seacomb to fetch Dr. Hillyard, the most important medical man in that quiet little town.

'Wallace is not so fresh as he might be, sir; you drove him rather fast last night.'

'Take Tarpan, then.'

This was a wonderful concession on the Squire's part. But Tarpan was the fastest horse in the stable, and Churchill was nervously anxious for the coming of the doctor. That heavy breathing might mean nothing—or it might——! He dared not think of coming ill—now—when he had built his life on new lines,—content to accept a future shorn of all that glorifies life, in the minds of worldings, so that he kept Madge, and Madge's fond and faithful heart.

Tarpan was brought out, a fine upstanding horse, as Hunter called him, head and neck full of power, eye a trifle more fiery than a timid horseman might have cared to see it.'

'He's likely to go rather wild in harness, isn't he, sir?' asked Hunter, contemplating the bay dubiously.

'Not if you know how to drive,' answered the Squire. 'The man I bought him from used to drive him tandem. Ask Dr. Hillyard to come back with you at once. You can say that I am anxious about Mrs. Penwyn.'

'Yes, sir. Very sorry to hear your lady is not well, sir. Nothing serious, I hope?'

'I hope not, but you can tell Dr. Hillyard I am anxious.'

'Yes, sir.'

Churchill saw the man drive away—the bright harness and Tarpan's shining coat glancing gaily between the pine trees as the dog-cart spun along the avenue—and then went back to his wife's room and sat by the bedside, and never left his post till Dr. Hillyard arrived, three hours later. Madge had slept all the time, but still with that heavy laboured breathing which had alarmed her husband.

Dr. Hillyard came quietly into the room, a small, grey-headed old man, whose opinion had weight in Seacomb and for miles round. He sat by the bed, felt the patient's wrist, lifted the heavy eyelids, prolonged his examination, with a serious aspect.

'There has been mental disturbance, has there not ?' he asked.

'My wife has been anxious, and over-fatigued, I fear, attending a dying servant.'

'There is a good deal of fever. I fear the attack may be somewhat serious. You must get an experienced nurse without delay. It will be a case for good nursing. I don't want to alarm you needlessly,' added the doctor, seeing Churchill's terror. 'Mrs. Penwyn's youth and fine constitution are strong points in our favour; but, from indications I perceive, I imagine that her health must have been impaired for some time past. There has been a gradual decay. An attack so sudden as this of to-day would not account for the care worn look of the countenance, or for this attenuation,' gently raising the sleeper's arm, from which the cambric sleeve had fallen back, the wasted wrist which Churchill remembered so round and plump.

'Tell me the truth,' said Churchill, in accents strangely unlike his customary clear and measured tones. You think there is danger ?'

"Oh dear no, my dear sir, there is no immediate

danger. With watchfulness and care we shall defeat that tendency towards death which has been described as symptomatic of all fever cases. I only regret that Mrs. Penwyn should have allowed her physical strength to sink to so low a point without taking remedial measures. That makes the fight harder in a sudden derangement of this kind.'

'Do you imagine that it is a case of contagious fever—that my wife has taken the poison from the woman she nursed last night?'

'Was Mrs. Penwyn with the woman before last night—some days ago, for instance?'

'No; only last night.'

'Then there can be no question of contagion. The fever would not declare itself so quickly. This feverish condition, in which I find your dear lady to-day, must have been creeping upon her for a week or ten days. The system has been out of order for a long time, I imagine, and some sudden chill may have developed the symptoms we have to regret to-day.

CHAPTER XVI.

'FOR ALL IS DARK WHERE THOU ART NOT.'

BEFORE the week was out Muriel was so far recovered as to be able to bear a long journey, and so tranquil as to render that journey possible. Her couch had been wheeled into a corner of the family sitting-room—she had been brought back into the household life, and her father had devoted himself to her with a quiet tenderness which went far to soothe her troubled mind.

The old hallucinations still remained. She spoke of George Penwyn as living, and she could not be brought to understand that the child who had been taken from her an infant was now a woman. She had little memory—no thought of the past or of the future—but she clung to her father affectionately, and was grateful for his love.

Maurice had made all arrangements for Muriel's

journey before leaving Cornwall, after his interview with Churchill. It had been settled that Martin should bring his sister to the neighbourhood of London, accompanied by Phœbe, as her attendant. This Phœbe was a bright active girl, quite able to manage Muriel. Maurice was to find pleasant apartments in the suburbs, where Muriel might be comfortably lodged. In less than twenty-four hours after his departure from Borcel he had telegraphed Martin to the effect that he had found pleasant lodgings in a house between Kentish Town and Highgate, a house with a good garden.

Three days later Muriel came to take possession of these lodgings, worn out with the long journey, but very tranquil. Her daughter was waiting to receive her on the threshold of this new home.

Very sad, very strange was that meeting. The mother could not be made to comprehend that this noble-looking girl who held her in her arms, and sustained her feeble steps, was verily the child she had been robbed of years ago. Her darling was to her mind still an infant. If they had placed some feeble, wailing babe in her arms and called it hers, she would have believed them, and hugged the impostor to her breast and been happy; but she did not believe in Justina.

'You are very kind to come,' she said, gently, 'and I like you; but it is foolish of them to say you are my child. I am a little wrong in my head, I know, but not so foolish as to believe that."

On one occasion she was suddenly struck by Justina's likeness to her father.

'You are like George,' she said. 'Are you his sister?'

Martin brought a famous doctor from Cavendish Square, one of the kindest of men, to see Muriel. He talked to her for some time, inquired into the history of her malady, and considered her attentively. His verdict was that her case was hopeless.

'I do not fear that her case will ever be otherwise than gentle,' he said, 'nor do I recommend any more restraint than she has been accustomed to, but I have no hope of cure. The shock which broke her heart shattered her mind for ever.'

Justina heard this with deepest sorrow. All that filial love could offer to this gentle sufferer she freely gave, devoting her days to her mother, while her nights were given to the public. None could have guessed how the brilliant actress—all sparkle and vivacity, living in the character her art had created —spent the quiet hours of her daily life. But she had Maurice always near her, and his presence brightened every hour of her life.

He had laid his case before his lawyers, and even the cautious family solicitor had been compelled to own that it was not altogether a bad case. What was his astonishment, however, when, three days later, he was told that Messrs. Pergament and Pergament had met his solicitors, examined documents, discussed the merits of the case, and finally pronounced their client's willingness to surrender the estate, in its entirety, without litigation.

‘ But I told Mr. Penwyn of his cousin's willingness to accept a compromise, to take half the value of the estate, and leave him in possession of the land,’ said Maurice.

‘ Mr. Penwyn elects to surrender the estate altogether. An eccentric gentleman, evidently.’

‘ Then the whole business is settled ; there will be no law suit.’

'Apparently not,' said the solicitor, drily.

Lawyers could hardly live if people were in the habit of surrendering their possessions so quickly.

Maurice called on Messrs. Pergament and Pergament, and explained to the head of that firm that the young lady for whom he was acting had no desire to exact her full claim under Squire Penwyn's will, that she would prefer a compromise to depriving Mr. Penwyn and his wife of house and home.'

'Very generous, very proper,' replied Mr. Pergament. 'I will communicate that desire to my client.'

Justina was horrified at the idea of Churchill Penwyn's renunciation. All her old distrust of him vanished out of her mind—she thought of him as generous, disinterested — abandoning estate and position from an exalted sense of justice.

'But it is not justice,' she argued, 'though it may be right according to my grandfather's will. It is not just that the child of the elder-born should take all. Maurice, you must make some one explain my wishes to Mr. Penwyn. I will not rob him and his wife of house and home. I cannot have such a sin upon my head.'

'My dearest, I fully explained your views to Mr. Penwyn.   He treated me with scornful indifference, and declared that he would fight for his rights to the last.   He has chosen to see things in a new light since then.   His line of conduct is beyond my comprehension.'

'There must be some mistake, some misapprehension on his part. You must see him again, Maurice, for my sake.'

'My dear love, I don't mind oscillating between London and Penwyn Manor for the next six weeks if my so doing will in the smallest degree enhance your happiness; but I do not believe I can make your views any clearer to Mr. Penwyn than I made them at our last interview.'

'My dear Justina,' interposed Mr. Elgood, pompously, ' the estate is yours, and why should you hesitate to take possession of it? Think of the proud position you will hold in the county; your brilliant table, at which the humble comedian may occupy his unobtrusive corner. And I think,' he added, with a conciliatory glance at Maurice, ' there is some consideration due to your future husband in this matter.'

'Her future husband would be as well pleased to take her without a shilling as with Penwyn Manor,' said Maurice, with his arm round Justina.

'Of course, my dear boy,—

> "Love is not love
> When it mingled with respects that stand
> Aloof from the entire point."

Shakespeare. You would take your Cordelia without a rood of her father's kingdom ; but that is no reason why she should not have all she can get. And if this Mr. Churchill Penwyn chooses to be Quixotic, let him have his way.'

'I will write to him,' said Justina. 'I am his kinswoman, and I will write to him from my heart, as cousin to cousin. He shall not be reduced to beggary because my grandfather's will gives me power to claim his estate. God's right and man's right are wide apart.

CHAPTER XVII.

For fifteen days and nights Churchill Penwyn watched beside his wife's bed with only such brief intervals of rest as exhausted nature demanded ; an occasional hour, when he allowed himself to fall into a troubled slumber, on the sofa at the foot of the bed, from which he would start into sudden wakefulness, unrefreshed, but with no power to sleep longer. Even in sleep he did not lose consciousness. One awful idea for ever pursued him, the expectation of an inevitable end. She, for whom he could have been content to sacrifice all that earth can give of fame or fortune, she with whom it would have been sweet to him to begin a life of care and toil, his idolized wife, was to be taken from him.

London physicians had been summoned, two of the greatest. There had been solemn consultations in Madge's pretty dressing-room, the room where she had been so utterly happy in the first bright years of her wedded life; and after each counsel of medical authorities, Churchill had gone in to hear their verdict, gravely, vaguely delivered,—a verdict which left him at sea, tempest-tossed by alternate waves of hope and fear.

There had come one awful morning, after a fortnight's uncertainty, when the great London physician and Dr. Hillyard received him in absolute silence. The little grey-haired Seacomb doctor turned away his face, and shuffled over to the window; the London physician grasped Churchill's hand without a word.

'I understand you,' said Churchill. 'All is over.'

His calm tone surprised the two medical men; but the man of wider experience was not deceived by it. He had seen that quiet manner, heard that passionless tone too often before.

'All has been done that could be done,' he said kindly. 'It may be a comfort for you to remember that in days to come, however little it lessens your loss now.

'Comfort!' echoed Churchill, drearily. 'There is no comfort for me without her. I thank you for having done your uttermost, gentlemen. I will go back to her.'

He left them without another word, and returned to the darkened room where Madge Penwyn's brief life was drifting fast to its untimely close, under the despairing eyes of her sister Viola, who from first to last had shared Churchill's watch.

But seldom had either of these two won a recognising glance from those clouded eyes,—a word of greeting from those parched lips. Only in delirium had Madge called her husband by his name, but in all her wanderings his name was ever on her lips, her broken thoughts were of him.

At the last, some hours after the doctors had spoken their final sentence and departed, those tender eyes were raised to Churchill's face, with one long, penetrating look, love ineffable in death. The wasted arms were feebly raised. He understood the unexpressed desire, and drew them gently round his neck. The lovely head sank upon his breast, the lips parted in a happy smile, and with a faint sigh of contentment, bade farewell to earthly care.

Tearless, and with his calm, every-day manner, Churchill Penwyn made all arrangements for his wife's funeral. The smallest details were not too insignificant for his attention. He opened all letters of condolence, arranged who, of the many who loved his wife, should be permitted to accompany her in that last solemn journey. He chose the grave where she was to lie—not in the stony vault of the Penwyns—but on the sunny slope of the hill, where summer breezes and summer birds should flit across her grave, and all the varying lights and colours of sky and cloud glorify and adorn it. Yet, in those few solemn days between death and burial, he contrived to spend the greater part of his time near that beloved clay. His only rest—or pretence of rest —was taken on a sofa in his wife's dressing-room adjoining the spacious chamber, where, beneath whitest draperies, strewn with late roses and autumn violets, lay that marble form.

In the dead of night he spent long hours alone

in that taper-lit bedchamber, kneeling beside the snowy bed—kneeling, and holding such commune as he might with that dear spirit hovering near him, and wondering dimly whether the dream of philosophers, the pious hope of Christians, were true, and there were verily a world where they two might see and know each other again.

Sir Nugent Bellingham had been telegraphed to at divers places, but having wandered into inaccessible regions on the borders of Hungary, to shoot big game with an Hungarian noble of vast wealth and almost regal surroundings, the only message that reached him had arrived on the very day of his daughter's death. He reached Penwyn Manor, after travelling with all possible speed, in time for the funeral, altogether broken down by the shock which greeted him on his arrival. It had been a pleasant thing for him to lapse back into his old easy-going bachelor life—to feel himself a young man again—when his two daughters were safely provided for; but it was not the less a grief to lose the noble girl he had been at once proud and fond of.

The funeral train was longer than Churchill had planned, for his arrangements had included only the elect of the neighbourhood. All the poor whom Madge had cared for,—strong men and matrons, feeble old men and women, and little children,—came to swell the ranks of her mourners, dressed in rusty black—decent, tearful, reverent as at the shrine of a saint.

'We have lost a friend such as we never had before and shall never see again.' That was the cry which went up from Penwyn village, and many a hamlet far afield, whither Madge's bounty had penetrated—where the sound of her carriage wheels had been the harbinger of joy.

Churchill had a strange pleasure, near akin to sharpest pain, as he stood in his place by the open grave on a sunless autumn morning, and saw the churchyard filled with that mournful crowd. She had been honoured and beloved. It was something to have won this for her—for her who had died for love of him. Yes, of that he had no doubt. His sin had slain her. Care for him, remorse for his crime, had sapped that young life.

A curious smile, cold as winter, flitted across Churchill's face as he turned away from the grave, after **throwing a** shower of violets on the coffin. Some among the crowd noticed that faint smile, wondered at it.

' Before **another week** has come, I shall be lying in my darling's grave.'

That was what the smile meant.

When he went back **to the Manor House,** Viola, deeply compassionating his quiet grief, brought his son to him, thinking there might be some consolation in the little one's love.   Churchill **kissed** the boy gently, **but** somewhat coldly, **and** gave him back to his aunt.

' My dear,' **he** said, '**you meant** kindly by bringing him to me, but it only pains me to see him.'

' Dear Churchill, **I** understand,' answered **Viola,** pityingly, ' but it will **be different** by and by.'

' **Yes,**' said Churchill, with a wintry smile, ' it will be different by and by.'

He had received Justina's letter—a noble letter, assuring him of her unwillingness to impoverish him or to lessen his position as lord of the manor.

'Give me any share of your fortune which you think right and just,' she wrote. 'I have no desire for wealth or social importance. The duties of a large estate would be a burden to me; give me just sufficient to secure an independent future for myself and the gentleman who is to be my husband, and keep all the rest.'

Churchill re-read this letter to-day, calmly, deliberately. It had reached him at a time when Madge's life still trembled in the balance, when there was still hope in his heart. He had not been able to give the letter a thought. To-day he answered it. He wrote briefly, but firmly,—

'Your letter convinces me that you are good and generous,' he began, 'and though I ask, and can accept nothing for myself, it emboldens me to commit the future of my only son to your care. I surrender Penwyn Manor to you freely. Be as generous as you choose to my boy. He is the last male representative of the family to which you claim to belong, and he has good blood on both sides. Give him the portion of a younger son, if you like, but give him enough to secure him the status of a gentlemen.   His grandfather, Sir Nugent Bellingham, and his aunt, Miss Bellingham, will be his natural guardians.'

This was all.   It was growing dusk as Churchill sealed this letter in its black-bordered envelope— soft grey autumn dusk.   He went down to the hall, put the letter in the postbag, and went out into the shrubbery which screened the stables from the house.

There had been gentle showers in the afternoon, and arbutus and laurel were shining with raindrops. The balmy odour of the pines perfumed the cool evening air.   Those showers had fallen upon her grave, he thought, that grave which should soon be reopened.

He opened a little gate leading into the stable yard.   The place had a deserted look.   Grooms and coachmen were in the house eating and drinking, and taking their dismal enjoyment out of this time of mourning.   No one expected horses or carriages to be wanted on the day of a funeral.   A solitary underling was lolling across the half-door of the harness-room smoking the pipe of discontent.   He recognised Churchill and came over to him.

' Shall I call Hunter, sir ?'

' No, I want to get a mouthful of fresh air on the moor, that's all.   You can saddle Tarpan,'

A gallop across the moor was known to be the Squire's favourite recreation, as Tarpan was his favourite steed.

' He's very fresh, sir.   You haven't ridden him for a good bit, you see, sir,' remonstrated the underling, apologetically.

' I don't think he'll be too fresh for me.   He has been exercised, I suppose ? '

' Oh, yes, sir,' replied the underling, sacrificing his love of truth to his fidelity as a subordinate.

' You can saddle him, then. You know my saddle ?'

' Yes, sir.   There's the label hangs over it.'

Churchill went into the harness-room, and while the man was bringing out Tarpan, put on a pair of hunting spurs, an unnecessary proceeding, it would seem, with such a horse as Tarpan, which was more prone to need a heavy hand on the curb than the stimulus of the spur.   The bay came out of his loose box looking slightly mischievous, ears vibrating, head restless, and a disposition to take objection to the pavement of the yard, made manifest by his legs. The Squire paid no attention to these small indications of temper, but swung himself into the saddle and rode out of the yard, after divers attempts on Tarpan's side to back into one of the coachhouses, or do himself a mischief against the pump.

'I never seed such a beast for trying to spile his money value,' mused the underling when horse and rider had vanished from his ken. 'He seems as if he'd take a spiteful pleasure in laming his-self, or taking the bark off to the tune of a pony.'

Away over the broad free expanse of grey moorland rode Churchill Penwyn. There had been plenty of rain of late, and the soft turf was soft and springy. The horse's rapture burst forth in a series of joyful snorts as he felt the fresh breeze from the broad salt sea and stretched his strong limbs to a thundering gallop.

Past the trees that he had planted, far away from the roads that he had made, went the Squire of Penwyn, up to the open moorland above the sea the wide grey waters facing him with their fringe of surf, the darkening evening sky above him, and just one narrow line of palest saffron yonder where the sun had gone down.

Even at that wild pace, earth and sea flying past him like the shadows of a magic lantern, Churchill Penwyn had time for thought.

He surveyed his life, and wondered what he might have made of it had he been wiser. Yes, for the crime by which he had leaped at once into possession of his heart's desires seemed to him now an act of folly; like one of those moves at chess which, lightly considered, point the way to speedy triumph, and whereby the rash player wrecks his game.

He had won wife, fortune, position; and lo! in little more than two years, the knowledge of his crime had slain that idolized wife, and an un-dreamed-of claimant had arisen to dispute his fortune.

The things he had grasped at were shadows, and like shadows had departed.

'After all,' he said to himself, summing up the experience of his days, a man has but one power over his destiny—power to make an end of the struggle at his own time.'

He had ridden within a few yards of the cliff. His horse turned, and pulled landwards desperately, scenting danger.

'Very well, Tarpan, we'll have another stretch upon the turf.'

Another gallop, wilder than the last, across the undulating moor, a sudden turn seaward again, a plunge of the spurs deep into the quivering sides, and Tarpan is thundering over the turf like a mad thing, heedless where he goes, unconscious of the precipice before him, the rough rock-bound shore below, the wild breath of the air that meets his own panting breath, and almost strangles him.

* * * *

Sir Nugent Bellingham waited dinner for his son-in-law, sorely indifferent whether he eat or fasted, but making a feeble show of customary hours, and household observances. Eight o'clock, nine o'clock, ten o'clock, and no sign of Churchill Penwyn. Sir Nugent went up to Viola's room. It was empty, but he found his daughter in the room which had so lately been tenanted by the dead, found her weeping upon the pillow where that placid face had lain.

'My dear, it is so wrong of you to give way like this.'

A stifled sob, and a kiss upon the father's trembling lips.

'Dear papa, you can never know how I loved her.'

'Every one loved her, my dear. Do you think I do not feel her loss? I have seen so little of her since her marriage. If I had but known! I'm afraid I've been a bad father.'

'No, no, dear. You were always kind, and she loved you dearly. She liked to think that you were happy among pleasant people. She never had a selfish thought.'

'I know it, Viola. And she was happy with her husband. You are quite sure of that?'

'I never saw two people so utterly united, so happy in each other's devotion.'

'And yet Churchill takes his loss very quietly.'

'His grief is all the deeper for being undemonstrative.'

'Well, I suppose so,' sighed Sir Nugent. 'But I should have expected to see him more cut up. Oh, by the way, I came to you to ask about him. Have you any idea where he has gone? He may have told you?'

'Where he has gone, papa? Isn't he at home?'

'No. I waited dinner for an hour and a half, and went in alone (learning that you were too ill to come down) and ate a cutlet. It was not very polite of him to walk off without leaving any information as to his intentions.'

'I can't understand it, papa. He may have gone to town on business, perhaps. He went away suddenly just before—before my dearest was taken ill—went one day and came back the next.'

'Humph,' muttered Sir Nugent. 'Rather un-mannerly.'

There was wonderment in the house that night, as the hours wore on, and the master was still absent, wonderment most of all in the stables where Tarpan's various vices were commented upon.

Scouts were sent across the moors—but the night was dark, the moors wide, and the scouts discovered no trace of horse or rider.

Sir Nugent rose early next morning, and was not a little alarmed at hearing that his son-in-law had not returned, and had gone out the previous evening for a ride on the moor.

It was just possible that he had changed his mind, ridden into Seacomb, and left Tarpan at one of the hotels while he went on by the train which left Seacomb for Exeter at seven o'clock in the evening. He might have taken it into his head to sleep at Exeter, and go on to London next morning. A man distraught with grief might be pardoned for eccentricity or restlessness.

The day wore on, as the night had done, slowly. Viola roamed about the silent house, full of dreariest thoughts, going to the nursery about once every half-hour to smother her little nephew with tearful kisses. His black frock and his artless questions about ' Mamma, who had gone to heaven,' smote her to the heart every time she saw him.

Sir Nugent telegraphed to his son-in-law at three clubs, thinking to catch him at one of the three if he were in London.

The day wore on to dusk, and it was just about

the time when Churchill had gone to the stables in quest of Tarpan yesterday afternoon. Viola was standing at one of the nursery windows looking idly down the drive, when she saw a group of men come round the curve of the road, carrying a burden. That one glance was enough. She had heard of the bringing home of such burdens from the hunting-field, or from some pleasure-jaunt on sea or river.

There was no doubt in her mind, only a dreadful certainty. She rushed from the room without a word, and down to the hall, where her father appeared at the same moment, summoned by the loud peal of the bell.

Some farm-labourers, collecting seaweed on the beach had found the Squire of Penwyn, crushed to death among the jagged rocks, rider and horse lying together in one mangled mass.

The trampled and broken ground above showed the force of the shock when horse and rider went down over the sharp edge of the cliff.

A fate so obvious seemed to require no explanation. Mr. Penwyn had gone for his gallop across the moor, as he had announced his intention of doing, and betrayed by the thickening mists of an autumnal evening, his brain more or less confused by the grief and agitation he had undergone, he had lost ken of that familiar ground and had galloped straight at the cliff. This was the conclusion of Sir Nugent and Viola, and subsequently of the world in general. The only curious circumstance in the whole business was the Squire's use of his spur, a punishment he had never been known to inflict upon Tarpan before that fatal ride. This was commented upon in the stable, and formed the subject of various nods and significant shoulder shrugs, finally resulting in the dictum that the Squire had been off his head, poor chap, after losing his pretty wife.

So, after an inquest and verdict of accidental death, Madge Penwyn's early grave was opened, and he who had loved her with an unmeasured love was laid beside her in that peaceful resting-place.

*   *   *   *   *

Justina did not deprive little Nugent of his too early inherited estate. A compromise was effected

between the infant's next friend, Sir Nugent Bellingham, and Justina's next friend, Maurice Clissold,
and the baby-squire kept his land and state, while
Justina became proprietress of the mines, the
royalties, upon which, according to Messrs. Pergament, were worth three thousand a year. Great
was the excitement in the Royal Albert Theatre
when the young lady who had made so successful
a *debut* in 'No Cards' retired, on her inheritance
of a fortune.

There was a quiet wedding, one November
morning, in one of the Bloomsbury churches—a
wedding at which Matthew Elgood gave the bride
away, and Martin Trevanard was best man—a
quiet, but not less enjoyable, wedding breakfast
in the Bloomsbury lodging, and then a parting, at
which Mr. Elgood, affected at once by grief and
Moselle, wept copiously.

'It's the first time you've been parted from your
adopted father, my love,' he sobbed; 'and he'll
find it a hard thing to live without you. Take
her, Clissold; there never was a better daughter
—and as the daughter, so the wife. She's a girl

in a thousand. "Ay, the most peerless piece of earth, I think, that e'er the sun shone bright on." God bless you both. Excuse an old man's tears. They won't hurt you.'"

And so, with much tenderness on Justina's side, they parted, the bride and bridegroom driving away to the Charing Cross Station, on the first stage of their journey to Rome, where they were to stay till the end of January. There had been a still sadder parting for Justina that morning in the quiet house between Kentish Town and Highgate, where the bride had spent the hour before her wedding. Muriel had kissed her, and blessed her, and admired her in her pretty white dress, and so they had parted, between smiles and tears.

When bride and bridegroom were comfortably seated in the railway carriage, travelling express to Dover, Maurice took an oblong parcel out of his pocket, and laid it in Justina's lap.

'Your wedding present, love.'

'Not jewels I hope, Maurice.'

'Jewels!' he cried, with a laugh. 'How should a pauper give jewels to the proprietress of flourishing tin mines? That would be taking diamonds to Golconda.'

She tore open the package with a puzzled look.

It was a small octavo volume, bound in ivory, with an antique silver clasp, and Justina's monogram in silver set with rubies—a perfect gem in the way of bookbinding.

'Do not suppose that I esteem the contents worthy the cover,' said Maurice, laughing. 'The cover is a tribute to you.'

'What is it, Maurice?' asked Justina, turning the book over and over, too fascinated with its outward seeming to open it hastily   'A Church Service?

'When one wants to know the contents of a book one generally looks inside.'

She opened it eagerly.

'A Life Picture! Oh, how good of you to remember that I liked this poem!' cried Justina.

'It would be strange if I forgot your liking for it, dearest. Do you remember your speculations about the poet?'

'Yes, dear, I remember wondering what he was like.'

'Would you be very much surprised if you heard
that he is the image of me?'

'Maurice!'

'I have given you the only wedding gift I had to
offer, love—the firstfruits of my pen.'

'Oh, Maurice, is it really me?   Have I married
a poet?

'You have married something better, dear; an
honest man, who loves you with all his strength,
and heart, and mind.'

*   *   *   *   *

Three years later and Maurice's fame as a poet is
an established fact, a fact that grows and widens
with time.   Mr. and Mrs. Clissold have built themselves a summer residence, a house of the Swiss
châlet order, near Borcel End, where Muriel lives
her quiet life, her father's placid companion, harm-
less, tranquil, only what Phœbe the housemaid calls
'a little odd in her ways.'

Justina and Viola Bellingham are fast friends,
much to the delight of Martin Trevanard, who con-
trives somehow to be always at hand during Viola's
visits to the châlet.   He breaks in a pair of Iceland

ponies for that lady's phaeton, and makes himself generally useful. He is Viola's adviser upon all agricultural matters, and has quite given up that old idea of establishing himself in London. He rides to hounds every season, and sometimes has the honour of showing Miss Bellingham the way—an easy way, for the most part, through gates, and convenient gaps in hedges.

The old-fashioned neighbours who admired Martin's mother as the model of housewives, indulge in sundry animadversions upon the young man's scarlet coat and Plymouth-made top-boots, and predict that Martin will never be so good a farmer as his father : a prophecy hardly justified by facts, for Martin has wrought many improvements at Borcel by a judicious outlay. The trustees of the estate have renewed Michael's tenancy on a lease of three lives, which will in all probability secure the farm to the house of Trevanard for the next half-century.

'Mr. and Mrs. Clissold have set up their nursery by this time, an institution people set up with far less consideration than they give to the establishment of a carriage and pair, but which is the more costly luxury of the two; and nurses and ladies at the châlet are sworn allies with the young Squire and his nurse from the Manor House, where Viola is mistress. Sir Nugent Bellingham comes to Cornwall once in three months for a week or so, yawns tremendously all the time, looks at accounts which he doesn't in the least understand, and goes back to his clubs and the stony-hearted streets with infinite relief.

Happy summer-tides for the young married people, for the children, for the lovers! Sweet time of youth and love and deep content, when the glory and the freshness of a dream shineth verily upon his work-a-day world.

THE END.

J. AND W. RIDER, PRINTERS, LONDON.